Let Sleeping Dogs Die

When Linus Rintoul is asked to look into the alleged age of a Kennel Club member—a point which calls in question the man's integrity—he refuses, but when he buys an appealing watercolour of a cow he finds himself drawn into an extraordinary imbroglio concerning changed identities, Nazi war-loot—and murder. It's an imbroglio in which the age of dog-breeding art-dealer Raymond March is crucial—but who is John Smith? And why does an attractive woman engaged in tracking down missing works of art lack even the most basic knowledge of her subject?

The trail leads the government vet from his Oxfordshire base to a fort in the Solent, where not everything proves to be quite what it seems . . .

by the same author

JUDGE AND BE DAMNED
DEAD SPIT
DOG'S BODY

JANET EDMONDS

Let Sleeping Dogs Die

THE CRIME CLUB
An Imprint of HarperCollins *Publishers*

First published in Great Britain in 1992
by The Crime Club, an imprint of
HarperCollins Publishers, 77–85 Fulham Palace Road,
Hammersmith, London W6 8JB

9 8 7 6 5 4 3 2 1

A catalogue record for this book is
available from the British Library

ISBN 0 00 232391 5

Photoset in Linotron Baskerville by
Rowland Phototypesetting Ltd
Bury St Edmunds, Suffolk
Printed and bound in Great Britain by
HarperCollins Book Manufacturing, Glasgow

AUTHOR'S NOTE

Of the four Spithead Forts, three are in private hands, one of them—Spit Bank—being a tourist attraction (and back on the market at the time of writing). The fourth, Horse Sand, still belongs to the Ministry of Defence. I have described Spit Bank as it is and Horse Sand differs from it in the ways described, though the superstructure and any references to its adaptation for domestic life are entirely figments of my imagination.

Janet Edmonds

CHAPTER 1

'They're monsters,' Beverley had said. 'Absolute monsters.'

Linus Rintoul had shaken his head and his smile had been unintentionally condescending. Dogs were dogs. Some were big and some were small and a few individuals of all sizes should have been strangled at birth, though, as often as not, if that fate had been handed out to their owners, the dogs would probably have turned out all right. Monsters were something else.

'A monster,' he had pointed out patiently, if pedantically, to the young vet who, for reasons incomprehensible to Linus, had decided to start her professional career at the Ministry of Agriculture, Fisheries and Food, 'is a misshapen animal or one made up of bits of other animals.'

'That's right,' she had replied cheerfully. 'They're monsters.'

So Linus decided to see for himself. The next time the quarantine kennels were due for an inspection, he'd take it on. In the meantime, out of curiosity, he looked the dogs up for himself. At least, he tried to. It wasn't as easy as he'd expected for the simple reason that no dog book he could find listed Slovenian Mastiffs.

Admittedly, the range of literature at his disposal was limited. There were veterinary textbooks, there were Is-This-Your-Dog wallcharts from drug and petfood manufacturers and there was the limited stock in Oxford's bookshops. Linus supposed it was hardly surprising that the breed didn't feature in the sort of general-appeal books stocked by places like W. H. Smith's. Dog-breeders these days imported all sorts of weird and wonderful things, mostly to enable them to get started in a breed on or very near the ground floor at a time in the breed's development when prices could make it very lucrative indeed. It could take years before some of the breeds reached the general dog-books.

They say owners get like their dogs. Linus's own companion was a Pit Bull Terrier to which he had given a home in a moment of weakness some years before, and if there was one characteristic he shared with Ishmael, it was a disinclination to let go once he had his teeth into something. It irked him not to be able to find anything out. He rang that obvious source of canine information, the Kennel Club.

'Sorry, it's not one of the breeds we recognize,' the girl on the information desk told him. 'I'm sorry, I can't help you.'

He rang John Chilson with whom he had been at vet school and the only member of the Kennel Club he knew personally.

'Never heard of it, but I'll tell you what: I've got to go up to Clarges Street next week. I'll see what's in the library there. There may be something in one of the foreign books.'

'You can't even make an educated guess about it?' Linus pressed him.

'No better a guess than you can. If it's a mastiff, it's likely to be big and if its origin is Central European there's a good chance it's a guarding breed—and they like them sharpish.'

'You're right,' Linus told him. 'I'd got that far myself.'

It wouldn't have surprised him if Chilson had forgotten all about it but he rang Linus back towards the end of the following week. 'Now there's a funny coincidence,' he said. 'These Slovenian Mastiffs.'

'You've discovered something?'

'Not a thing. Not a mention anywhere. But we've had an application to recognize the breed from someone who's just imported a couple. Not a hope in hell, of course: if they're not already recognized by the ruling body of the country of origin, we don't want to know. Bit awkward, really, because in this case the importer's a Member.'

'Doesn't that make a difference? The right handshake and all that?' Linus asked with calculated naïvety.

'Now that's naughty,' Chilson replied, though he chuckled. 'No, it doesn't. The only breed we've made an exception for in recent years was the Anatolian Karabash, and we had statements from the Turkish Ambassador and God knows who else to verify the breed's existence. It won't happen again, and it certainly won't happen with anything that sounds a potential liability. Believe me, sighs of relief have been heaved at the Kennel Club because it refused to recognize those ghastly dogs you've got.'

'It's not the dogs, it's the owners,' Linus told him.

'Very true, and there's an awful lot of bloody stupid owners out there. Now tell me, how come you're suddenly interested in these Slovenian things at this time?'

'Only idle curiosity. There's a couple in quarantine in this area. Very probably the same couple you've heard about. The girl who did their last inspection says they're monsters. It struck me as rather a drastic verdict so I thought I'd find out for myself.'

Linus could almost see his friend's ears prick up. 'Nasty, are they?'

'She didn't say so. Didn't seem unduly bothered, so they can't have been. I picked her up on the word and my guess is they're just rather ugly.'

'I don't suppose there's any chance of your looking at them yourself?' Chilson asked.

'No problem—I'd intended to anyway. Any particular reason?'

'You're a level-headed sort of chap. I'd quite like your personal opinion on the breed. On the QT, you know.'

'I'll give you a ring.'

'We can do better than that. Why not treat yourself to a day in Town?'

'Now why should I do that?' Linus asked, amused and mystified since he knew Chilson lived no closer to London than he did himself.

'Call it Public Relations or something. I'll buy you lunch at the Kennel Club and we can chat. What do you say? The food's good,' he added encouragingly.

'You've just twisted my arm.'

'Can we say Thursday week?'

'Fine.' It struck Linus that Chilson was extraordinarily anxious to have his opinion on the breed but he couldn't imagine why, especially since the KC appeared already to have made up its mind. Perhaps he'd learn more over the promised lunch.

Linus didn't find them ugly at all, though he'd have been the first to admit that his judgement wasn't necessarily the same as anyone else's. They were certainly huge. Without a doubt, the biggest dogs he'd ever seen. The male, the larger of the two, was at least the height of a large Great Dane but with none of the svelte, elegant lines of that breed. 'Mastiff' was an apt breed description. The nearest comparison Linus could make was with the Pyrenean or perhaps the Newfoundland but with the extra substance commensurate with the extra height. They had the same long, wavy, rather silky coat. He wasn't smitten with the colour which he supposed a dog-breeder would describe as 'blue' and he particularly disliked the fact that, in common with most blue dogs, the eye colour was yellow. It lent a predatory, leonine look to the face and this calculating sharpness of expression was enhanced by the fact that both dogs had been cropped. This was not the partial cropping designed to give an erect ear, as in the Dobermans and Boxers on the Continent, but the almost total removal of the ear-flap, leaving just a tiny piece standing. There was no doubt that it wasn't the natural size or shape of the ear: the narrow edge of hairless leather bore witness to that.

'D'you think they're meant to be cut as short as that?' he asked David Thelwall, the vet who owned the kennels.

'According to the owner, it's to prevent wolves having something to hang on to,' David replied. 'Apparently three men hold the half-grown dog down so that each ear in turn can be laid out on a block and a fourth man chops it off with a sharp axe.'

Linus winced. 'Nasty.'

'Very. I gather the survival rate isn't too high, either: the peasants don't waste good money on antibiotics.'

'Temperament?'

'They've been no problem here. Not exactly outgoing, hail-fellow-well-met. A bit aloof and not, I suspect, particularly obedient. I wouldn't want to get on the wrong side of one, but, to be fair, while they've been here they've shown no sign of having a wrong side.'

'And the owner?' Linus glanced at the card outside the kennel to refresh his memory. Raymond March.

David shrugged. 'Not one of the forthcoming ones. Some owners tell you their life story; others sign in, visit their dogs and sign out. March comes into that category.'

'You don't happen to know whether he's a member of the Kennel Club?'

'No idea. It's not impossible: he's certainly not petsy-wetsy and I think I heard him mention another breed. Always comes here with a minder—a much younger man whom Ruth says reminds her of those gorgeous creatures in Leni Riefenstahl's film of the Berlin Olympics.' David chuckled. 'Not necessarily a minder, I suppose. Could be part of the dog world's gay mafia. It might fit. At all events, Mr March isn't short of the odd bob or two. Right up your street, as a matter of fact.'

Linus stiffened. They were friends but there were limits. 'I hope you're not still referring to the gay mafia?' he said.

Thelwall stared at him in astonishment. 'Good God, no. I meant his business. He's got an art gallery in Henley. Thought you might know it.'

'I may know it by name but if it's in Henley it'll be out of my reach. Still, maybe I'll look in, just out of curiosity.' He glanced back at the dogs. 'Henley, eh? I don't think the neighbours are going to be very happy when they see these.'

'Oh, they're not destined for Henley. It seems March has another place in the Solent. They're going there as guards.'

'Well, at least if they go berserk on the Isle of Wight, they can't reach the mainland. I'll mention it to Chilson.'

'Chilson?'

'Chap I was at vet school with. KC member who didn't know anything about Slovenian Mastiffs, either. As a matter of fact, I'm having lunch with him in a couple of weeks. At the Kennel Club,' he added, unable entirely to suppress the merest smidgin of a boast.

Thelwall laughed. 'Bully for you. I've heard it's good.'

'I'll report back,' Linus promised.

Linus made a detour through Henley on his way back from inspecting a flock of dairy sheep. His first glimpse of the gallery told him his instincts had not been wrong. It was likely to be way above his touch. Still, there was no harm in looking.

The window was occupied in solitary splendour by one late eighteenth-century French landscape that verged on the romantic and had been painted by a lesser-known but first-class artist. The carefully composed and generous folds of a white velvet curtain constituted the setting for this jewel. There was, of course, no price.

Linus was quite surprised to be able to walk in without buzzing for the door to be unlocked, but soon realized that the catch had been discreetly released as soon as his intent to enter had become apparent.

The gallery was larger than its exterior suggested and its owner had resisted the temptation to cram the walls with all his stock. Each white plane carried just one carefully lit picture, but because the gallery was an old building composed of a succession of fairly small rooms, there were quite a few pictures to see. They were all good and one fell into that category of blandness which Linus castigated as 'furnishing pictures'. There were several he would have been happy to have on his own walls though none he yearned for—which was, he thought, probably just as well in view of their likely prices.

There was no mistaking the minder Thelwall had mentioned. Ruth's quoted description was extremely apt. The tall, blond Adonis who moved with the coordination of an athlete could indeed have stepped straight out of Riefenstahl's film. Linus could almost imagine him hurling the discus. Only when the young man moved his head was perfection seen to be marred by the thin white line of an old scar along his cheekbone. Linus was unsure whether to regret it as an imperfection or to be secretly pleased at proof that the young god was actually human.

Linus had moved on to a second picture before an older man emerged from the back of the gallery and approached him. The timing could have been random; somehow Linus didn't think it was.

This could only be Raymond March. For one thing, he had the indefinable air of proprietorial authority. For another, he wore the distinctive Kennel Club tie.

He was dressed informally but not casually. Not for Mr March the jeans and checked shirts currently *de rigueur* among the owners of provincial galleries. His grey flannels and Harris tweed jacket proclaimed him the English country gentleman—except that English country gentlemen, even those no longer young, had usually moved on these days to the ubiquitous jeans. The effect here was slightly incongruous and more than slightly old-fashioned. Linus glanced across at the discus-thrower. He was wearing jeans so dark they were almost black and an impeccably white polo-necked sweater that set off his tan to perfection. The garments were casual. The effect was not. Linus could understand why they might be taken for a homosexual couple, yet somehow, though he would have been hard put to it to explain why, he didn't think they were either homosexual or a couple.

'Do you see anything to interest you?' March asked. The voice was very English, too. It was, Linus thought, one of those that owes rather more to elocution lessons than to upbringing.

'Plenty,' he replied. 'Unfortunately, I've a strong suspicion my bank manager wouldn't play ball.'

The man shrugged imperceptibly. 'Don't reject something just on that score,' he said. 'We can usually reach some sort of accommodation.'

'I don't think you and he would see eye to eye on what was acceptable,' Linus told him ruefully. 'I like paintings and I know enough about current prices to know when I'm out of my financial depth. If there were something here I couldn't live without—well, maybe then I'd stick my neck out and ask, but there isn't. You've some superb stuff here but nothing so far that—how can I put it?—speaks to my condition quite strongly enough.'

Raymond March smiled and for the first time there was a hint of warmth about him. 'Browse to your heart's content,' he said. 'Not many art lovers come through that door. Investment is what most of them are after. If there were any justice in the world, it would be the art lovers who'd have the money to buy, not just investors.'

'I'll drink to that,' Linus told him.

Just off the third room he saw the little office from which March must have emerged. There was a small Victorian armchair just inside it and two small dogs were curled up in it, sound asleep. Linus wondered what Beverley would have made of dogs with skins patched in blue and pink and quite hairless except, so far as he could see, for a tuft of white hair on the top of their heads, their paws and at the end of the only tail currently visible.

'Unusual,' he commented.

'Chinese Crested. I breed them. They fit the image.'

Linus refrained from commenting that if fewer people used dogs to fit what they perceived to be their 'image', there would be fewer canine misfits. These bizarre creatures were hardly in the same category as some of the macho breeds that were associated with problems. He wondered what sort of 'image' the Slovenian Mastiffs were intended to boost. 'Do you have any others?' he asked.

March looked surprised. 'Yes, several. You need more than two to establish any sort of kennel.'

'But just the one breed?'

'If one's going to make a success of something, it doesn't pay to diversify too much. That's why I stick to late eighteenth-century/early nineteenth-century paintings and a few drawings. I know my field and don't go outside it.'

'Very wise,' Linus agreed. He found himself wondering how old the man was. Not young and probably a lot older than he looked. Certainly a lot older than Linus himself, yet his face seemed to lack what Linus could only call the lived-in look most people acquire with age. He peered closely at a tiny painting of the castle of Chillon. 'The subject's become hackneyed,' he commented, 'but on this scale it suddenly acquires a new freshness.'

'My view precisely,' March told him and Linus caught a sudden glimpse of a very heavy gold curb-chain bracelet which sat oddly with the English-country-gentlemen look.

By no means a straightforward man, our Mr March, he thought.

When he left, the discus thrower opened the door for him and Linus had the feeling he was watched all the way back to his car. He'd been rather longer than he'd intended and although he'd left himself a fair bit of room, he now found himself pretty well boxed in by a blue car behind. Fortunately he still had some room to manœuvre in front and then he was glad to note that the woman behind was backing those few necessary inches. He raised his hand in acknowledgement as he pulled out, muttering as he did so a few uncharacteristic remarks about women drivers. Good looks, he thought savagely, don't excuse careless parking.

CHAPTER 2

The Kennel Club façade was bland and uninteresting. It was the sort of tasteful building that should never have been allowed. Ugly would have been preferable. Ugly would at least have made the passer-by think. Linus sighed and wondered what Victorian delight this one had replaced.

His glance fell on the life-sized bronze foxhound just inside the glass door and his appreciative heart lifted. The bronze had nothing to apologize for.

He pushed open the inner door and went in. 'John Chilson's guest—Linus Rintoul,' he told the dark-haired girl at the desk.

'Oh yes. I've heard about you,' she said and her interested glance suggested this was no mere pleasantry. 'Take the lift to the fourth floor. He'll meet you in the Club Room.'

Linus did as he was told and found a room that accorded so precisely with his image of a gentleman's club that he had to remind himself this one was no longer exclusive to his sex. There were several interesting paintings on the wall, but only one, of a sleeping greyhound, was of an artistic merit commensurate with its probable listed value. There was no sign of Chilson, so he sat down in one of the ubiquitous leather armchairs and helped himself to a copy of *The Times* from a nearby table where the range of papers and magazines was surprisingly eclectic, considering it didn't, thank God, cater for the lowest common intellectual denominator.

The steward brought him some coffee which he said would go on Chilson's account and Linus decided this was a life to which he could very easily become accustomed. There wasn't a great deal in the paper of any particular interest, though his eye was caught by a small paragraph referring to the fact that a Rembrandt drawing, known to have been among the vast hoard of Nazi loot which had disappeared at the end of the War, had turned up in a Japanese collection. Argument appeared to be raging as to whether it was genuine, and should therefore be returned to its original owner, or a fake. Either way, Linus thought, the Japanese collector was the loser. He couldn't truthfully say that his heart bled for him.

He had moved on to the pie-in-the-sky delights of *Country Life*'s property pages before Chilson put in an appearance. He held two pages out to him as he approached. 'Which shall I go for?'

Chilson studied the castle in Caithness which had a roof and the Georgian estate outside Dublin which didn't and shook his head. 'Long way to cycle to work,' he said.

Linus sighed as if that clinched it. 'You're right, of course. I've had some coffee. Hope you don't mind.'

'Not a bit. Sorry to have kept you waiting. G and T?'

Chilson fetched the drinks himself and said, as he handed one to Linus, 'What happens to you after 1992?'

'Why should anything happen to me?' Linus was genuinely startled.

'Oh, I don't know. End of trade barriers and all that. You know.'

'No, I don't know. I'm a vet, remember? Not a business man.'

'But a lot of work has to do with . . . oh, import/export. That sort of thing.'

'Not all that much.' Linus looked at his companion intently. 'You're fishing, Chilson. Come on, what's this all about?'

Chilson shifted uneasily in his chair and then laughed grudgingly. 'I never was particularly good at subtlety,' he admitted. 'What we'd like to know is whether quarantine will be abolished.'

'Wouldn't everyone?' Linus replied. 'Why ask me, for God's sake? I'm just about at the bottom of the pecking order where these things are concerned. You need the Minister or the Secretary of State or whatever the top man calls himself these days. And being a canny politician, I very much doubt if he'll be daft enough to commit himself either way.'

'You haven't had a memo or anything about it?'

'By the time anything like that filters down to me, it'll be common knowledge,' Linus told him. 'All I can tell you is that those of us who will have to deal with rabies when it comes want to see quarantine retained, a fact which I promise you will cut no ice at all with any politicians here or in Europe. There's an element of fatalism about it anyway, thanks to the Tunnel. No matter what the politicians say about safeguards—about metal grids to keep vermin out, and all that—once it's in use, it's only a matter of time. It'll most likely come in via some stupid or careless or criminally irresponsible pet owner because Customs won't be able to do thorough checks and the French at the other end don't give a damn. Alternatively we wait until rats gnaw through the safety grids. Don't politicians realize the little beasts can chew through metal? If the rats aren't rabid, they'll be followed by foxes that are. Then God help us.'

'The anti-dog lobby's loud enough as it is,' Chilson commented, 'and largely irrational. Give them a case of rabies to get their teeth into . . .'

'You're preaching to the converted,' Linus reminded him. 'Mind you, it'll be the end of the Animal Rights movement—they won't be so keen on protecting anything with a pretty face when one bite might kill.'

'You're a cynic.'

'You think so? So far as I'm concerned, if there are rights for rabbits and foxes, then there are rights for cockroaches and rats. I haven't heard anyone protesting about any attempts to eliminate them. Even the anti-vivisection lobby concentrates on the "nice" animals. But rats are highly intelligent creatures. They must suffer just as much as rabbits.'

'So you're opposed to the idea of animals' rights?'

'As a matter of fact, I'm not. I'm opposed to inconsistency.' He looked at his watch. 'I don't want to be rude, but you did say lunch.'

Chilson led the way into the adjoining dining-room and they sat at a table tucked away in a corner, some distance from the handful of other diners. It was, Linus observed, the perfect place from which a conversation would not be heard. The menu was limited but interesting and Linus opted for the dressed crab and the roast guinea-fowl. Both, he was to note, were superb.

Conversation remained general at first, from which Linus deduced that his host was entirely convinced that he could throw no light on the subject of quarantine. Finally Chilson turned the talk into more particular channels.

'Did you ever go to see those Slovenian Mastiffs?' he asked.

'As a matter of fact, I did.'

'What did you make of them?'

'Their sheer size makes them impressive. I don't like their yellow eyes and I certainly didn't like the way most of their ear-flaps had been chopped off. Still, that won't happen to their off-spring.'

'And apart from that?'

'You mean temperament? Fine. Thelwall described them as stand-offish and not hail-fellow-well-met. He said he doubted if they were very obedient. I'd be inclined to endorse that opinion. They didn't welcome my presence but they raised no objection to being examined.'

'Guard dogs?'

'Probably. I wouldn't like to say whether they'd limit themselves to a warning bark or whether they'd follow it up. To be honest, I don't think it would matter much: just the sight of them would be all the deterrent most people would need.'

'But you wouldn't want to see them in the wrong hands.' It was a statement rather than a query.

'Of course not. I don't want to see anything in the wrong hands. Jack Russells are pretty nasty if they go to people who think small is cute.'

'I don't suppose you happened to bump into their owner, Raymond March?' Chilson asked.

Linus, who knew perfectly well he had never mentioned the owner's name because it would have been unethical if he had, debated how best to answer this 'have-you-stopped-beating-your-wife' question. Since Ministry records indicated that there were only the two Slovenian Mastiffs in quarantine at the present time and no import licences for others had yet been applied for, and since March had already asked the KC to recognize the breed, it seemed a bit pedantic to stick to the absolute letter, especially since it could be argued that a comment to a fellow vet was not necessarily a breach of ethics. Best perhaps just to accept that they both knew whom they were talking about.

'Not at the kennels. Our inspections aren't done during visiting hours. Thelwall told me he had an art gallery in Henley, so I popped in.'

'And?'

'Beyond my price range, I'm afraid. Some very nice stuff, though. Very nice.' It amused Linus to comment on the aspect of the visit he guessed held the least possible interest for Chilson. 'Late eighteenth/early-nineteenth-century and mostly European. Several good French pieces.'

'Did you meet March?' Chilson persisted impatiently.

'Harris tweed and grey flannels and an accent to fit. Carefully acquired, I'd say. Had a couple of Chinese Crested in his office. Said he breeds them.'

'Very successfully. What age would you put him at?'

Linus considered the matter. 'Tricky. I'd say he has to be older than either of us, quite possibly a lot older, but there was something about him which makes it difficult to be more precise. I'd have to fall back on the phrase more usually applied to women: "of uncertain age".'

'Ah!' Chilson said triumphantly, almost as if he had caught his friend out. 'You've put your finger on it. You've nailed our problem dead centre.'

Linus was completely bemused. 'You've lost me,' he said. 'What the devil are you talking about?'

Chilson looked about him in the furtive manner of a spy in a second-rate thriller and lowered his voice. 'We have a rule here that no one over seventy-five can stand for the General Committee and March is putting himself up for it. Some people think he's not been quite up front about his age.'

'So what's the problem? Ask him.'

'We have. In a way. He had to sign a declaration that the information he gave was accurate, and it had to include his date of birth.'

'You're beginning to sound like the Inland Revenue,' Linus commented. 'What age did he put? Twenty-four?'

'Don't be daft. No, sixty-five.'

Linus thought about it. 'All of that, I'd say.'

'You think he's more?'

Linus shrugged. 'Who am I to judge? I can believe sixty-five. I think I'd believe sixty-eight more easily. Either way, it's a long way short of seventy-five, so what's the hassle?'

'The point is not whether he's too old for the General Committee—I don't think anyone's suggested that he is—but that he declared the wrong age.'

'If he did,' Linus pointed out. 'So what if he is older than he admits? All it proves is that he's vain. Women do it all the time.'

'Not in the Kennel Club, they don't,' Chilson said firmly.

'You reckon?' Linus was cynical. 'You've a touching faith in human nature. How many of your members are married to each other?'

'I don't know. Quite a few, I imagine.'

'A quarter? A fifth?'

'I've never checked but that sounds about right.'

'And how many of those do you fondly imagine could produce valid marriage certificates?'

'Now you're being ridiculous! Most of them.' Chilson saw the trap. 'No, all of them, for God's sake!'

'You were right first time. As a statistical probability, ten per cent of them, give or take a percentage point, aren't. Does it matter?'

'Well, no—yes—I don't know.'

'So what does March's age matter until and unless he

uses a falsification to stand for a committee for which he might be ineligible?'

'I take your point but it doesn't work like that. We have to have integrity on committees. We have to know we can trust those standing for them. And a question has been raised about March's age.'

'Ask him to produce a birth certificate.'

Chilson looked shocked. 'That would look as if we didn't trust him,' he protested.

'But you don't,' Linus pointed out.

'Good God, man, you can't ask a chap to produce his birth certificate! What would it look like? Besides, he couldn't.'

'What do you mean, he couldn't?'

'The Club's solicitors have already gone through the records. There's no trace.'

Linus stared at him in silence for a few moments. 'You don't think there's just a hint of double-think in all this?' he suggested. 'It's apparently "not done" to ask someone to produce his birth certificate but it's OK to pay lawyers to dig around behind his back. That smells rather nasty to me.'

'But don't you see? If the searches proved it was all as he claimed, he'd never have the unpleasantness of knowing there'd been some doubt.'

'And that makes it all right? Sorry, I don't agree.' Linus cut himself a piece of Stilton and pointed the knife across the table at his companion. 'I'll tell you something. When I met March I have to say I didn't take to him. Several things about him seemed—oh, I don't know—a bit phoney, I suppose. I wrote him down as a poseur. But right now I'm warming to him by the minute. Besides, maybe he was born abroad.'

'We thought of that but it doesn't get us very much further forward.'

'I'd have thought most countries recorded births by the early years of this century,' Linus said thoughtfully. 'Certainly if they were part of the British Empire.'

'You wouldn't like to dig around into it, I suppose?'

'You suppose right. I've better things to do with my time. Pay a private detective if it matters that much to you. Personally, I think it would be a whole lot easier to write to him, say the Club's very sorry this question has been raised, but it has and the Club has to look into it and would he please send you the relevant documentation. That way the whole thing's open and above-board. The Club has made a reasonable request and if he doesn't supply it or it doesn't tally with what he's said, then you really do have a problem of integrity and you have to decide what to do about it. Tell me, what makes people so sure he's older than sixty-five—apart from a sort of gut-uncertainty like mine?'

'They say he looks as if he's had plastic surgery.'

'An accident? Burns?'

Chilson shook his head. 'No. Purely cosmetic, I gather. Apparently it's too smooth—a bit like those American ladies whose mouths are permanently smiling.'

'Mmm. I know what they mean. It's not smoothness, exactly, so much as a lack of the character lines that come with age. Yes, I think that's what I didn't like about him. Life's little troubles had not left much mark. Still if someone wants to waste his money on cosmetic surgery, it's up to him. It's not a form of vanity I'd give a second thought to myself. I'd rather spend the money on a good picture.'

'So you won't help?'

'No. For one thing, it's not my field. For another, I honestly can't see it matters all that much. If you want my opinion, which you probably don't, you're going to Birmingham by way of Beachy Head. Much quicker to go by

British Rail from Paddington. The direct route, and all that. Faster and less hassle.'

Linus spoke the truth when he told Chilson that official inspections of quarantine kennels were made outside visiting hours but he couldn't pretend the conversation about Raymond March hadn't raised more questions than it answered and he had little compunction in asking Thelwall to let him know when the Slovenian Mastiffs could expect another visit from their owner. He would be intrigued to see whether his view of March had changed.

So, when Thelwall left a message at the office that March would be coming next day, Linus rearranged part of his schedule and found himself in the north of the county, heading from the Banbury stockyard to Thelwall's isolated establishment hidden—and muffled—behind its screening hedge of well-grown conifers. Over the last four or five years, Ruth Thelwall had planted, apparently at random, a selection of native trees on the roadward side of the hedge and, while the trees themselves were far from mature yet, the underplanting of hazel, hawthorn and dog-rose had grown sufficiently to disguise the severe line of the hedge almost to the point of making it unrecognizable as such. In another two or three years there would appear to be nothing but coppice over there, the actual access track being already unobtrusively tucked away. In short, where once one had a good view of the whole kennels and its rather ugly bungalow from the road, now one saw a chimney and a roof-ridge and not much else.

One person who had as clear a view as possible was the driver of a blue car parked on the wide verge. Linus supposed it was a better place for a picnic than some he had seen. It beat a main road lay-by, for instance. Still, only half a mile further back in the direction from which the car had presumably come, there was a charming bluebell wood.

The best of the blooms were over now but there was still enough of the azure ground-haze to guarantee oohs and ahs of delight from Sunday motorists. He was surprised the woman hadn't stopped there.

He glanced at her as he swung into the track. It was a handsome enough face to make him glance in her direction again. He had a vague feeling he'd seen her before. This was perfectly possible. His work took him over a large area and he was always lunching in different pubs. He might very well have seen her before. Or, more likely, someone of the same physical type. He'd often observed how people frequently fitted one type or another and it could be quite misleading.

Just before he rounded the corner into the concealed car park, he heard an engine start up and glanced into his mirror to see the blue car pull on to the road and away.

He guessed that the sleek and spotlessly black two-seater Mercedes in the car park belonged to Raymond March. It fitted somehow, even though an aged estate would have sat better with the Harris tweed and flannels. He could just imagine the discus thrower at the wheel. Linus smiled to himself. Presumably they used something else to take the dogs to shows. He thought about it. A Volvo estate was a possibility. Or a Range-Rover. Something a little flash, like the gold curb-chain. He parked and went in.

March and the discus thrower were both in the office when Linus entered and both glanced up at the newcomer. The older man frowned with a recognition he couldn't quite place. The discus thrower had no such problem. He looked at Linus and his face went deliberately blank. It crossed Linus's mind that, if March continued not to place him, the young minder might not necessarily enlighten his ignorance.

Linus saw no point in beating about the bush. 'Fancy meeting you here,' he said. 'Linus Rintoul, though you won't know the name. I came into your art gallery the other day. You *do* have a gallery in Henley, I take it?' It seemed diplomatic not to be too positive.

March smiled. 'Of course. I thought you were familiar but it's sometimes difficult when you meet someone out of their usual context, if you follow me.'

'I know what you mean,' Linus assured him. 'Except that this *is* my usual context and art galleries are the occasional diversion.'

Now that the idea of cosmetic surgery had been planted in his mind, he was surprised it hadn't occurred to him before. That was exactly what the man looked like. Linus was hardly qualified to pass an opinion on the matter, yet he thought any surgery had been rather more than a tuck or two to tighten the jaw-line. The face was oddly characterless. It was rather fleshy, with a few lines but nothing like as many as one would expect on a man of his admitted age, much less an older one, and the nose was incongruously perfect. It was a little too short and a little too straight to balance the rest of the face. The chilly blue eyes were just a shade too close together, though that could hardly be laid at a surgeon's door. It was surprising, Linus thought, what a difference fractions of inches could make in a face. The discus thrower's facial proportions were perfect—and owed their perfection to nothing but Nature. March's hair was more white than grey and baldness was obviously not a family trait. A mane was the trite comparison that sprang to Linus's mind. If fitted perfectly. A mane of thick, white waves worn rather longer than was currently fashionable and, Linus thought, having more in common with the gold curb-chain than with the Harris tweed, but then again, perhaps he was being unduly harsh. So far as age was concerned, he would certainly place the man above his original estimate of sixty-five maybe, and sixty-eight more probably; but how much more he was unwilling to commit himself. If he were being charitable, he would say the man lived well and had worn well.

'He's being unduly modest,' David Thelwall butted in. 'He's got quite a nice little collection.'

March smiled the polite smile of the connoisseur who had learned from experience that most people's 'quite nice' was not necessarily his.

'It's not limited to period or theme or even country,' Linus said. 'I buy what I like and I've been fortunate to find the odd piece at a time when the artist wasn't much thought of and was consequently within my reach.'

'The best way to do it,' March remarked. 'Anything in particular?'

'I'm rather pleased with one of Dulac's illustrations to *The Sleeping Beauty*. That was a real find. And I've a pleasant drawing by Landseer which I picked up about thirty years ago.'

'Then you have indeed got "quite a nice collection",' March said.

Linus demurred. 'I can't claim there's anything else comparable,' he said.

'Don't be modest. Drop into the gallery again some time. I've some drawings that might well appeal and they needn't be exorbitant.'

'That's an important consideration,' Linus laughed and decided it was time to move the conversation on. At the gallery, March had denied any breeds other than Chinese Cresteds. 'I didn't realize we had any little hairless things in here,' he said. 'Or are you just making a preliminary visit?'

'I've a couple of Slovenian Mastiffs in.'

'Oh yes. Impressive beasts. Shall you start breeding those?'

'Possibly. A lot will depend on how I get on with them.

I may have problems getting them recognized but that doesn't worry me unduly.'

'Won't it make it more difficult to sell the progeny?' Linus asked.

March shook his head. 'I don't think so. It would cut out the show fraternity, of course, but if they make as good guards as I hope, there shouldn't be a problem.'

'Sounds as if Henley will love them.'

'Not Henley. I've a little place in the Solent. They're going there. No neighbours and it's escape-proof.'

'Sounds ideal.'

Ruth Thelwall came over just then. 'Your office had rung, Linus. Before you go back to the office, will you look at some pigs at Bampton.'

'Why? What's the problem?'

'They said they'd rather you went with an open mind but don't leave it till tomorrow.'

March and the discus thrower—Linus was still uncertain what the nature of their relationship might be—followed him out but whereas their Mercedes burst into perfectly maintained life at the first turn of the key, Linus's rather more aged estate needed coaxing. He turned on to the access track as their tail-gate disappeared down the road but he was just in time to see a familiar blue car pull out of the concealment of a field entrance and follow them. Linus then realized that it wasn't so much the car, which was nothing if not nondescript, which he recognized, as the driver. He was quite sure it was the woman whom he had taken to be picnicking when he arrived. It had been quite an extended picnic. And why move just a few yards down the road? He shook his head. Whichever way you looked at it, people were a funny lot. Give him cows every time. Or dogs.

CHAPTER 3

It was never easy to park in Henley. On this occasion Linus's luck held and he found a space not far from the gallery. There was no reason at all to notice a slightly shabby dark red saloon which pulled in a few spaces down, and only the fact that there was something faintly familiar about the woman who got out attracted Linus's attention to her at all. That, and the fact that she was decidedly good-looking. 'Handsome' had been the word that had sprung to mind when he had seen her outside the kennels and it was an appropriate one. She was tall and dark-haired with dark eyes in a strong-featured face. No one would ever call her pretty. She was, he decided, more than merely attractive without achieving beauty in the conventional sense. She threw over her shoulders a dull crimson poncho edged with a matching fur that might or might not be genuine. At this distance it was impossible to tell. The effect was elegant and very, very Henley.

He crossed the road to the gallery and this time when he entered Raymond March came forward to greet him as he would an old and valued customer. Linus hoped the warmth of the greeting didn't foreshadow the price of any pictures he might produce but guessed it was a faint hope at best.

March escorted him to the back of the gallery and indicated banks of drawers of the sort in which maps are customarily stored, with a broad, deep top so that the contents may be studied with the minimum risk of damage to their edges.

Some were drawings, some were engravings, a few were considerably earlier than March's stated range. All were

Continental and, except for an engraving after the younger Cranach, none were by artists whose names were known to Linus. There was no particular significance in that, of course: minor European artists were hardly his field if, indeed, he could claim to have one. But he knew enough to know that what he was looking at was good. Very good. He was unsure whether to be glad or sorry that he fell in love with none of them.

The drawings exhausted, March opened a further drawer which contained a small number of unframed watercolours. These were mostly of a much later date and one among them caught Linus's eye.

Although he was a vet, he normally found depictions of animals infinitely resistable but this was different. It showed a cow with her calf and what caught Linus's attention was not only that the cow was a real cow rather than the usual stylized one, but that the tender look in her dark brown eyes as she turned her head towards a totteringly new-born calf was clearly painted from life, and, more than that, painted with a love and understanding not often accorded to representations of domestic livestock. It was lovely and he wanted it.

'How much?' he asked.

March named a price which made Linus blanch and the dealer immediately knocked the customary ten per cent off. Linus knew that was a standard opening move but it still left reality too high.

He shook his head. 'Sorry,' he said. 'I'd love it, but at that price—or, to be quite frank, at anything near it—not in a month of Sundays.'

The dealer propped the picture up on a stand so that Linus couldn't easily lose sight of it and led him over to a chair by the office door. The chair faced the stand.

'Have a small drink and we'll discuss it,' he suggested. 'Let me guess. G and T?'

'I'm not sure a stiff brandy isn't more in order,' Linus said ruefully. 'But yes, G and T will be fine.'

Looking back on it afterwards, Linus had to admit that when it came to selling pictures, March was an expert. Not only did he know his field but he was an extremely shrewd judge of a customer. Linus, who loved the cow more every time he looked at her, had only two defences against him: his knowledge of his own financial limitations and the fact that he knew pictures of farm livestock, no matter how good, did not find a ready market.

Finally they reached a figure which Linus knew was within his reach—just, and bank manager permitting. Not that he expected any problems on that score: it wouldn't be the first purchase the bank had helped him with. March knew he was almost home and played the trump card that he guessed would finish the game.

'And of course, I get it appropriately framed for you,' he said.

Linus knew perfectly well that the right frame added enormously to the cost and that choosing that frame was an art in itself. Normally he went to Richard Adams, in Witney, whose eye was unerringly accurate but Linus had no doubt at all that he could leave the selection to March.

'Have you any idea how long it will take? I don't come to Henley all that often. Obviously, I'll make a trip in to fetch it but it won't be a case of popping in when I'm passing to see if it's ready.'

March got out his diary. 'A couple of weeks. Maybe three,' he said. He glanced up. 'I don't suppose you go to the shows?'

'Not regularly, but it has been known. Why?' Linus asked, surprised at such an apparent irrelevance.

'We could bring it to Bath if you were going to be there on the same day.'

'It smacks a bit of going to Birmingham by way of Beachy

Head, don't you think?' Linus said doubtfully. 'I'd find it a lot easier to pop in here when it's ready.'

'Of course, but that would mean waiting for it. You see, I close the gallery for most of May so that we can do the Championship shows: Birmingham, Scotland, Bath and Southern Counties all come in quick succession. And then—though I don't usually make too much of a noise about it—I have quite a profitable little sideline in canine pictures; models and memorabilia. I don't run the stall myself, of course, but I keep it supplied. It's a useful outlet for all sorts of things that come my way. I'll be taking several paintings to Bath so yours won't pose any special problems and if you could get there, too, it would save you having to wait until I open up here again.'

It made sense, but Linus was still doubtful. 'Isn't it risky?' he asked. 'Transporting pictures along with dogs, cages and equipment? I'd have thought things would be easily damaged, not to mention the security aspect.'

March tapped the side of his nose and grinned. 'Not the way I do it. It will be totally safe. Trust me.'

Linus was intrigued in spite of himself. There was no denying a trip to Henley would be much more convenient. He glanced at the cow again. On the other hand, he did want to see her on his walls as soon as possible and Bath would be a nice day out, so why not? 'Sounds a good idea,' he said and, while March wrote down details of the date and venue—which, like many dog shows, was far removed from the city which gave it its name—he decided to fish a little. 'Are you a local man?' he asked.

March looked faintly surprised. 'Local? No. Henley's a good place for this sort of business. It's not where I'd otherwise choose to live.'

'Of course. I remember. You've a place on the Isle of Wight, I think you said. A case of keeping in touch with your roots. I'm a Bristol man myself. Always enjoy going back.'

March handed him the slip of paper. 'I think you'll find that clear enough. I've written our benching numbers at the top. Look us up when you arrive and we'll take it from there.'

Linus was out of the gallery before he realized that his brief fishing trip had been totally unproductive. Not even a nibble.

He crossed the road immediately outside and had turned towards the row of parking bays when he caught sight of a familiar female figure in the pretty pink and white tea-room almost immediately opposite the gallery. He hesitated before deciding that a cup of coffee was just what he needed. A cup of coffee and a cream doughnut to ease the shock of the amount of money to which he'd just committed himself. His bank manager would probably have suggested it might be wiser to save that little extra expense, but his bank manager wasn't here. Linus pushed open the door and went in.

He wasn't at all sorry to find it pretty well packed out. Most of the customers were middle-aged, middle-class women enjoying a break from spending their husbands' hard-earned cash; some were young, jeans-clad yuppie mothers and there was a brace of retired couples. The husbands were the only other men in the place. And then there was the dark-haired woman near the window; there were no empty tables and hers was the only one with one customer, which was happily fortuitous.

'Do you mind?' he asked, indicating one of the empty chairs.

She obviously did but a glance over her shoulder revealed no more obviously available seat so she managed a polite smile and said, 'Of course.'

She was, Linus decided, about thirty-five and handsome

was still the right word. He particularly noticed her hands which were slender and well-cared for, with beautifully shaped, unpolished nails. She wore no wedding ring, he noted with approval, only a signet ring on her little finger, a large gold oval set with malachite, its dark green beauty unmarred by any engraved emblem. She was a woman to interest any man even without the intrigue of her appearances in places where March could be expected to be. It crossed Linus's mind that he had seen her on a third occasion: he rather thought she was the woman who had boxed him in on his first visit to March's gallery. Today's car was red. On both previous occasions it had been blue. OK, so lots of families ran two cars but they weren't usually of roughly similar size, age and nondescription. Definitely intriguing.

What's more, though she might not remember him from the first occasion—if, indeed, it had been she—she would certainly remember him from outside the kennels and she must have seen him come out of the gallery even if she hadn't seen him go in. And since he didn't think it was too far-fetched to assume she was watching March, it was also reasonable to assume that not only had she seen Linus but would have taken particular note. He would act on that assumption.

He waited until he had given his order to the waitress, a plump, middle-aged woman who confided that it gave her a real pleasure to find a man who wasn't bothered about his cholesterol.

'If you're going to go, you're going to go and you might as well go happy, is what I always says,' she confided. 'I like a nice drop of cream, meself, and jam doughnuts just aren't the same, are they?'

Linus agreed and when she'd gone, he glanced across at his companion.

'I suppose I ought to introduce myself,' he said. 'Linus Rintoul.'

She raised one eyebrow. As a gesture intended to depress pretension, it was remarkably effective and Linus felt himself wilt. 'Indeed?' she said. 'I can't imagine why.'

He resisted the temptation to retort that it had been his parents' choice. 'Our paths do seem to cross quite a lot,' he said instead.

'Do they? I hadn't noticed.'

The waitress returned with Linus's order and put it in front of him. 'You wrap yourself round that, dear,' she told him. 'I do like to see a man who enjoys his food.'

As she left the table, Linus caught the tail-end of a smile on the face opposite. He grinned in reply. 'Not the sort of waitress who makes you feel you've stepped out of your class,' he commented.

She laughed reluctantly. 'It's usually waiters who have that effect, I find. Some of them have turned it into an art form.' She paused. 'Didn't I see you come out of the gallery over there?'

Linus sighed. 'Yes, and I suppose my bank manager would tell me the price of this indulgence ought to go towards off-setting the loan I'm going to ask for.'

'You bought something?' She sounded surprised. 'It looks such a terribly expensive place.'

'A touch above my pocket, you mean?'

He was quite pleased to have discomfited her. Her composure had been rather daunting. Linus knew perfectly well she hadn't meant to sound rude but if embarrassment made her a little more human, he'd use it.

She flushed. 'I'm sorry. That sounded rude. I didn't mean it like that.'

'That's all right, I'm not offended. As a matter of fact, if it had been what you meant, it would have been absolutely spot-on. It *is* expensive and almost everything in it is way beyond my reach.'

'But not quite everything.'

'No, not quite everything. Do you collect?'

'When I was a child I collected stamps. That was a long time ago. I think one has to be fairly settled to collect seriously. After all, there has to be somewhere to put one's efforts. Even if they're not suitable for display, they have to be stored.'

'From which I infer you're not settled?'

She smiled—rather distantly, Linus thought. 'My work takes me all over. There isn't much opportunity to put down roots.'

'Sounds interesting. What do you do?'

She was immediately evasive. 'I think most people would find it rather tedious. I suppose it's a cross between public relations and market research. What about you?'

Linus decided this was not his day for successful fishing. 'I'm a vet, but not in general practice, which is how most people see the job. I'm MAFF—I work for the government.'

'And what does that entail?'

'A lot of it is purely advisory but we oversee the running of abattoirs and stockyards, keep a check on quarantine establishments, that sort of thing.'

He was very conscious of the fact that her wariness had subsided, her tenseness had relaxed: once he had explained his presence in the two places where March also happened to be, he had explained also a connection closer than coincidence.

The reaction of most women when they learnt of his job was to look quite blank, say 'How fascinating' and then glaze over if he made the mistake of going into any details which, since he enjoyed his work, he was inclined to do. This woman was different. She made no pretence.

'I'm sure you love it but it sounds horribly bucolic to me. I'm city born and bred. The nearest I get to meat is what comes out of the freezer, and that state of affairs suits me very well indeed.'

Linus made some noncommittal reply about her not being unique in that respect and then drank some coffee to give himself time to think. Public relations and market research were two areas of activity which sounded extremely vague to the man-in-the-street. They could also be held to encompass very well indeed the functions of a private detective. The puzzle was solved. Chilson had passed on his suggestion and here she was, though Linus felt bound to admit that he couldn't quite see how keeping an eye on March himself was going to throw any light on his date of birth.

'So the Kennel Club decided to hire someone after all,' he said.

She looked a bit taken aback, but that was to be expected. 'I'm not sure I follow.'

'Very discreet,' Linus said, smiling approvingly. 'Don't worry, my acquaintance with March is purely a business one. I probably shan't see him again except when I collect my picture.'

'And when will that be?'

'He suggested bringing it to Bath show—dog show, you understand. He breeds dogs. But of course, you know that.'

'It seems an odd place to pick up a picture, especially one that's quite pricey.'

'That's what I thought, but apparently he closes the gallery down in order to do several dog shows, and that way I don't have to wait. It seems he sometimes supplies less important pictures to some of the fine art stands at dog shows.' Linus thought it better, in view of March's own reservations, not to say the man had a stall of his own. 'So he's going there with other pictures anyway.'

'It sounds very odd to me. Can you trust him, do you think?' She looked quite flatteringly worried on Linus's behalf. 'After all, you're spending quite a lot of money, I gather.'

'I shan't pay for it until I collect it,' Linus assured her, 'and then it won't be with cash. One doesn't—a small holding deposit is all one lays out initially.'

'That sounds safe enough,' she agreed. She watched him eat his doughnut and suddenly giggled. 'I'm sorry. It's terribly rude to laugh but you've got a bit of cream on the end of your nose.'

Linus hastily wiped the end of his nose with his napkin. 'Is that better?' She nodded. 'It must have looked ridiculous.'

She considered the matter. 'No, not ridiculous, more endearing, really.'

The choice of word startled Linus. It also gave him courage. He liked the company of women but had very little confidence in his ability either to initiate or maintain relationships. A failed marriage behind him didn't help. Still, the word she'd used was 'endearing'.

'I don't suppose you'd consider having dinner with me some time?' he ventured.

She hesitated. 'I'd like to. It's a matter of finding an evening when I can be sure to be free.'

Linus presumed she must be billing the Kennel Club for overtime or unsocial hours, or whatever they called it in her line of work. 'You name the evening and I'll give you my phone number. Then, if something turns up to keep you away, you can let me know.'

She was happy with this arrangement, but declined his suggestion that he should pick her up. This was, Linus supposed, sensible enough these days, though he regretted the climate of violence and mistrust that made it necessary. She agreed instead to meet him at the Farmhouse

Restaurant at Lew which she said she'd have no difficulty finding. Linus gave her both his home and office numbers and wrote down his name to save her the embarrassment of having to admit she'd forgotten it. 'I'd better have your name, too,' he said. 'Otherwise a message from the office won't make sense.'

'Of course. Greentree. Miriam Greentree.'

'Unusual,' he said. 'Like an American Indian. There used to be a ballerina. Maria Hightower—something like that. She was an Indian.'

Miriam laughed. 'Well, I'm not. I'm English born and bred. Jewish, but English. My parents fled here from Germany in 1933—they saw the writing on the wall, despite the rest of the family assuring them they were being alarmist. They simply translated the name into English. They felt it was safer. I wish they hadn't. I'm proud of my heritage.'

'There's nothing to stop you changing it back,' Linus pointed out.

'I've thought about it but they're still alive—unlike the relatives who stayed behind—and they'd rather I didn't. They're convinced it would be dangerous. In any case, Linus Rintoul isn't exactly in the Bill Bloggs category.'

'Thoroughly Irish, which I'm not,' Linus told her.

He drove back to the office with a feeling of exultation that was strong enough to overcome the rising tide of panic that always followed close behind the purchase of a picture which he knew he couldn't really afford.

'My, we have come back in a good mood,' commented Lisa, the office's secretary. 'Found yourself a bit of crumpet?'

'For a good secretary, you really do have an exceptionally vulgar turn of phrase from time to time,' he told her affably.

She chuckled. 'Doesn't mean I'm wrong though, does it? Anyway, why shouldn't you enjoy yourself? After all, you'll soon be dead.'

'Thank you very much. For what it's worth, my girl, and as you will undoubtedly find out in time if no one strangles you first, the fact that you get older on the outside doesn't mean you feel any older on the inside.'

'Goodness me, we *are* feeling our oats today. And before you go galloping off round the paddock just for the fun of it, I need your records for last week. For all the evidence I've got of your activities, you might have been on a seven-day binge.'

Linus dropped the sheets on her desk on his way out. 'I've bought a picture,' he told her. 'I love it, but now I'm going home to have a good strong whisky before I tackle my bank manager.'

The Farmhouse was unusual in offering a set dinner and no menu. This wasn't nearly as limiting as it seemed because the soup was always unusual, the sorbet made with fresh fruit, the *hors d'oeuvres* trolley contained over twenty choices, the *entrée* consisted of a choice between two roasts and a pie, and there were thirteen items on the sweet trolley. Then there was cheese and biscuits and coffee. The fixed price was well within the reach of a man who had just paid rather more for a painting than he ought to have allowed himself to have afforded, and only the wines were extra. Linus always made a point of buying English wines if they were listed. People were inclined to denigrate them but they were, in his opinion, every bit as good as the best German ones and a great deal better than most.

They were shown to a table in the Victorian-style conservatory where they were served by girls in long Laura Ashley frocks and little mob-caps. It was a bit twee for Linus's taste but not enough to detract from the excellent food. Miriam certainly enjoyed the food and Linus was pleased to see she tucked in with gusto, with no nonsense about 'dieting tomorrow'. The conversation, while moving beyond the general, avoided mention of art galleries, the Kennel Club or anything on either side that could be remotely interpreted as fishing. As a consequence, both of them relaxed and enjoyed the evening.

They were well into the sweet when Linus was hailed by David Thelwall and his wife Ruth. 'Fancy seeing you here,' Thelwall said.

Linus resented the inference that he rarely dined out. 'If anyone's surprised at bumping into each other, it's me. Twenty-four-hour attendance at the kennels doesn't allow you to get out together very often.'

'Sometimes we make the effort,' Ruth told him. 'This is our wedding anniversary so we got in a kennel-sitter.' She looked inquiringly at Miriam and Linus made the introductions.

'We do all have a marginally common interest,' he went on. 'Miriam's interested in the career of our Mr March.'

Miriam made no comment and because he was looking at the Thelwalls as he spoke, Linus didn't see the mingled surprise and annoyance on her face.

'He collected those Mastiffs today,' Thelwall said. 'Can't say I'm sorry. Those two dogs never put a foot wrong and never gave any sign that they might, and yet . . . I don't know. I'm just glad they're not living next door to me.'

Linus glanced across at his companion. 'At least you're not going to have to hang about in field entrances in darkest Oxfordshire any more,' he said. Her answering smile was polite but distinctly frosty and the atmosphere had thawed but little by the time they had finished their coffee and brandy and were on their way out to the car park.

'Thank you for dinner,' Miriam said when she had found her keys. 'The meal really was delicious.'

'I'm glad you enjoyed it.' Linus hesitated. 'Enough, I hope, to repeat the experience.'

She looked him steadily in the eye. 'Yes—and no,' she said.

'And what's that supposed to mean?'

'Broadly speaking, I'd be very happy to have dinner with you again, but not if you're going to discuss my business with every Tom, Dick and Harry we bump into.'

'Thelwall isn't any Tom, Dick or Harry,' Linus protested. 'I only mentioned it because he knows the man, too.'

'I appreciate that but what if those dogs hadn't left his care today? What if next time March visited he was asked about me or asked—jokingly, you understand—if there was a woman watching him from across the road? What then?'

Linus felt himself flush and hoped it didn't notice in the moonlight. 'I'm sorry. I didn't think. I suppose it would rather queer your pitch.'

'And then some,' she said with more feeling than Linus thought the situation warranted.

'At least we know that can't happen now,' he said. 'Still, it was an unfortunate slip and I apologize. There's not much more I can do about it, is there? Will you have dinner with me again?'

She seemed to be hovering on the brink of a refusal and Linus was bracing himself to accept it gracefully prior to kicking himself when he was alone, but she changed her mind.

'I think I'd enjoy it,' she said at last. 'Especially if you'll be careful what you say and to whom.'

'It's a promise,' Linus assured her and made a mental note to find a restaurant where they were unlikely to bump into any of his acquaintances, thereby minimizing the likelihood of another unintentional gaffe. Much as he liked women, he did not seem to be one of those men to whose door they beat a path, so it behoved him to tread carefully when he had found one who was not only herself good-looking, intelligent and good company, but who found him interesting enough to want to see him again even though he had demonstrated an unfortunate ability to put his foot in it with gusto.

CHAPTER 4

Chilson had warned Linus that the Bath show had a well justified record for being very, very wet. 'Take your wellies and your tow-rope,' he had said when Linus told him he was going. 'It's not unusual for everyone to have to be towed out of the car park at the end of the day.'

Since, like most vets, both items went with him everywhere, the admonition was unnecessary and when Linus got up, he decided it was probably going to be superfluous as well. The weather in Oxford was perfectly splendid; the day bore all the hallmarks of being precisely the sort of day one would choose on which to take an attractive woman for a drive in the country.

Miriam was coming, too. They had dined out a couple of times and had lunched together once and when Linus suggested she come with him to pick up his picture, she had agreed. She hadn't leapt on it with glee, exactly, but Linus had the feeling—which he admitted was probably due as much to wishful thinking as to perspicacity—that she had been hoping he would ask and simply didn't want to appear too eager.

He still had no idea where she lived. He didn't even know whether it was in the city. She had avoided giving him her phone number ('I often don't bother to answer it, anyway. So many calls these days are . . . dubious') and he soon discovered she wasn't in the book. Directory inquiries were no help at all because he didn't have her address and even when he pointed out that her surname was more than a little unusual, they still said they couldn't even tell him if she was ex-directory unless he could provide the address. She had insisted on meeting him at whichever restaurant he chose and that meant, of course, that he couldn't take her home.

It annoyed him more than somewhat. Surely she knew him well enough by now to realize that he was no mad axe-man, and not even a man likely to push his luck beyond its limits? Such secrecy was not normal, and although he knew it didn't really matter where she lived, the fact that she was, to put it mildly, reticent about it, made it assume an importance it didn't really warrant. As a consequence, and although he despised himself for it, after one very pleasant evening he decided to follow her home.

Trailing vehicles without being observed is not a skill required of vets, not even those employed by the government, and Linus soon discovered it was a skill he lacked.

They had eaten at the Fox at Bix and Linus who, now he came to think about it, was usually the first to leave the car park, rooted around on the floor of the car as if searching for his keys or a glove or something of that sort. It required the skills of a contortionist to do this while still keeping an eye on the car park so that he knew when Miriam left.

She finally drove off and headed down the hill towards Henley. Linus gave it a few moments and then pulled out after her, behind another car that was fortuitously travelling the same road. This, he knew from occasional TV programmes, was what plain clothes detectives always did.

He began to suspect that either TV lied, or detectives both official and private were more adept than he. Obliged to stop behind the car in front at a major junction just before the town itself, he watched two cars turn into the road behind Miriam's disappearing tail-lights. By the time he had followed the bend of the one-way system along the riverbank to the traffic lights, she had beaten the red and turned left, while he was three cars back, waiting for them to change.

He too turned left over the bridge, but did so in the certainty that he had lost her and, since there was still no sign of her by the time he reached the junction that gave him a choice between the M4 and the M40, he took the latter back to Oxford. So she lived south of Henley. Big deal. He was a vet, not a sleuth and if he had any sense, he told himself, he'd stick to what he knew in future.

She had come back to his house in Osney Mead, however, just the once, after their lunch, for coffee. Full stop. Still, it was better than nothing, though her continued reticence did make him wonder if it were her way of telling him something.

He convinced himself that the projected trip to Bath would mark the end of her caution, but she had again declined being picked up from her home.

'Much easier if we meet somewhere,' she had said. 'There's a Little Chef on the A34, where it meets the M4. That should suit us both.'

It did, but Linus would have preferred a detour if it might herald a relationship closer than mere acquaintance.

The weather continued to hold as they turned off the M4, skirted Chippenham and headed westwards through warm limestone villages and along tree-lined roads. It was as cosy a landscape as the Cotswolds and the fact that it's charms were obvious in no way diminished them. Before long, they had turned into the winding lanes that led to the showground. The beauty of the scenery was less easy to appreciate here simply because they joined a line of estate cars, hatchbacks, vans and transits, all moving steadily in the same direction and each with its load of dogs, some loose, some caged. The line slowed, crawled, stopped.

'I hoped I'd time it to miss the rush,' Linus told his companion.

'We probably did too well on the motorway,' she said. 'Either that, or these people left it a bit late.'

That may well have been the case because after they had been stuck for a good five minutes with only the occasional creep forward to relieve the monotony, they began to be overtaken by exhibitors who had abandoned their cars to their partners and were walking to the showground rather than risk missing their classes. Most of them were carrying their dogs.

'For heaven's sake, haven't those dogs got legs to walk with?' Miriam asked with the exasperated amusement of an outsider.

'There's no pavement and the grass verges are almost certainly still wet,' Linus replied.

'So? Are pedigree dogs that delicate?'

'No need to sound so scornful,' he told her. 'They're not delicate at all. Far from it in most cases. No, a lot of work has been put into getting those coats exactly right. Grass is wet, and it stains. So does damp earth. Presentation matters at dog shows and it's well worth carrying the dog a few yards if it will preserve that presentation as near to perfection as possible. It's no different from any other beauty competition—Miss World, for instance.'

'I've no time for beauty contests,' Miriam said sharply. 'They're degrading to women.'

It didn't surprise Linus that she should hold that opinion. There was a certain earnestness about Miriam Greentree, a lack of frivolity, that made it inevitable. 'Maybe they are, but that's beside the point. It's still presentation that counts. They don't parade with their hair in rollers or their faces unmade-up.' He paused to move smoothly a further ten yards closer to their goal. 'You ought to go to an agricultural show,' he went on. 'Cows, pigs, sheep—they're all laundered and blow-dried and scissored to perfection.'

She turned and stared at him in disbelief. 'You're pulling my leg.'

Linus shrugged. 'You don't have to believe me. Go and see for yourself. You won't see a muddy udder at an agricultural show.'

A scarcely perceptible iciness crept into the atmosphere and Linus guessed she didn't altogether appreciate his choice of example. He had used it because it had seemed the most apt, not for any innuendo that might be read into it. He tended to forget that people whose lives were not tied up in livestock of one sort or another, who only saw meat in the supermarket and milk in bottles, were totally lacking in the earthly realism that farmers, vets and stockmen took for granted. Perhaps the gulf between him and this handsome woman was genuinely wider than he liked to think—and perhaps she was more aware of it than he.

Eventually they had edged far enough forward to be able at least to make sense of the delay. This was due to the fact that vehicles were entering the showground from opposite directions and had to filter through a gate too narrow to take two abreast. For some reason the police seemed to be giving priority to the other lot. Even as he thought this, Linus smiled to himself. They probably did no such thing. It was most likely an illusion, like the one leading to the belief that bread always falls butter-side down.

They were inside at last, and when they were, Linus could see that the organizers would have problems very quickly if it rained. The ground was soft and already beginning to be churned up—and this was the first of four days. No wonder there were a couple of strategically placed tractors handy.

By the time the car was safely locked up and they were in the showground itself, judging was well under way and since Linus was aware of no particular urgency in his mission, he was happy to loiter by the rings. He had no idea of the finer points of the dogs he was looking at but that didn't mean they weren't interesting and their handlers, in their infinite variety, were even more so. It didn't seem to be an opinion shared by Miriam, who was constantly looking restlessly about her.

'You're not enjoying this,' Linus said at last. 'Is there something else you'd rather do?'

'No, not at all,' she replied, a little too quickly. 'It's just all so very different from anything I've been to before. Aren't you going to do anything about your picture yet?'

'I suppose I'd better make contact,' he agreed. 'They won't welcome more than that until their breed's finished —and as long as that picture's in their hands, it's their responsibility and I don't have to pay for it. Once I've picked it up, we go. March may choose to take risks. I don't. Let's find some coffee.'

As luck would have it, one of the rings they passed on their way to the refreshment tent was just filling up with the first class of Chinese Cresteds. Linus paused by the ropes. 'This is March's breed,' he said. 'I wonder if he's in this class.'

He was, his shock of carefully shaped leonine white hair topping houndstooth checks and cavalry twill. Not just the English country gentleman, Linus thought, more the ex-army English country gentleman. He needed a haircut and a flat cap to complete the picture more accurately. Linus found himself surreptitiously moving his head through funny angles to see whether the gold curb-chain was still there. It was: an even greater incongruity when coupled with the ex-army image. There really was something about the man that wasn't quite right, or maybe Linus's problem was that he just couldn't stand a man who was as vain as this one clearly was, and was further irked by the sight of someone who aimed at one image but let it conflict with another. The hair and the chain went together.

Linus suspected they reflected the true Raymond March.

The art dealer glanced up from the puppy he was handling and looked towards the judge who was just leaving his table to view his line-up. March's eye strayed over the judge's shoulder and caught sight of Linus and he nodded a brief acknowledgement.

'That's all right, then,' Linus said. 'He knows I'm here. We'll look him up when they've finished.' He bent over a woman sitting just in front of them at the ringside. 'Excuse me,' he said. 'How many of these are entered?'

'About sixty-five,' she told him.

Linus straightened up. 'That gives us well over two hours,' he told Miriam.

'How can you be sure?'

'Simple. You calculate on a basis of two minutes per dog and most judges take a bit longer. On the other hand, there are always some absentees. No, two hours, quite possibly two-and-a-half, should see them through.'

They made their way towards the refreshment tent but coffee was still further delayed because, as they passed the veterinary tent, Linus caught sight of John Chilson's familiar figure.

'Is there such a thing as a show at which you're *not* in the veterinary tent?' he asked.

'Only the ones where I'm in the beer tent. What brings you here?' He glanced past Linus to Miriam and grinned. 'Ah, I see. You do have a genius for picking good-looking dog-breeders. I wish I could find them.'

'Miriam Greentree—John Chilson. And she's not a dog-breeder. I don't think she's ever been to a dog show before in her life.'

Chilson smiled at her in a way that might have been paternal had he been able to keep the merest hint of a leer out of it. 'Then take my advice and don't let yourself get hooked,' he told her. 'Dog shows can take over your life.'

'No danger of that,' she told him. 'I've more than enough on my plate as it is.'

Linus was puzzled. He had more than half expected Chilson to say, 'So *you're* Miriam Greentree. Nice to meet you.' After all, he was a member of the Kennel Club and had seemed to be taking a fairly active role in trying to solve the March mystery. Linus wouldn't even have been surprised to learn that they'd met—someone must have briefed her, after all. Yet he could have sworn Chilson had not only never met her but had never heard her name before. It wasn't as if it were a name one would easily forget. Then his brow cleared. The Kennel Club had probably brought in a company of which Miriam was just an employee. He had no idea how such firms worked but it seemed quite likely clients were not necessarily given the names of those working on their affairs.

'We're here to pick up a picture,' Linus went on. 'From your friend March, as a matter of fact.'

'Funny place for such a transaction,' Chilson commented. 'Where did it come from? Fall off the back of a lorry?'

'I very much doubt it.' Linus laughed, but uneasily. It had seemed odd to him, too, though Chilson's explanation hadn't occurred to him.

Then Chilson was looking past them. 'Can I help you?' he said.

Both Miriam and Linus turned and found themselves looking at the discus thrower.

He was as beautiful as ever, dressed this time in spotless white jeans and a black polo-necked sweater. He was staring at Miriam and transferred his gaze to Linus with an effort. 'Mr March asked me to catch you,' he said and Linus realized with a small shock that this was the first time he had heard him speak. The timbre of the voice fitted the rest of the picture but the accent was odd. There were definite, though slight, American overtones to it but there was something else as well. It wasn't the mid-Atlantic accent picked up by English emigrants. No, it was closer to the accent of a European who had been taught English by an American teacher. It irritated Linus because he couldn't quite place the European part of the accent.

'I saw him in the ring. I thought it would be more diplomatic to come back later.'

The discus thrower inclined his head and glanced involuntarily at Miriam once more. She seemed unaware of this. 'Mr March said after the judging would be fine. He said he guessed you'd want to be off.'

'I certainly shan't be leaving it unattended in the back of my car,' Linus agreed. 'About two hours, I imagine. I'll come to the benches.'

'I'll tell him.' Adonis glanced again at Miriam and was gone.

Chilson watched him go. 'Maybe I was wrong about March. If I was, he's another one who knows how to pick them.'

Linus would have enjoyed the next couple of hours a lot more if he hadn't been increasingly conscious that this wasn't Miriam's idea of a good day out. Her interest in the various trade stands was cursory. Linus didn't expect her to be fascinated by leads or nail-clippers but her interest in knitwear, in waterproofs and in antiques seemed no greater. Even the novelty of discovering just how great a diversity of goods was available at such an event plainly failed to enthral. Linus found it rather depressing and he realized that, apart from the fact that she had used to collect stamps as a child, he knew nothing whatever about her tastes or interests. Miriam was very good indeed at keeping a conversation going on a purely superficial, 'social' level, so that by the end of an evening one felt one had enjoyed oneself and yet would not have learnt one single thing about her. It wasn't simply a case of not knowing whether she preferred Bach to Brahms, or Beiderbecker to both, but of whether she had a family and where she grew up. She had talked a lot but she had said nothing. On the other hand, she had also drawn quite a lot out of him. Most people, Linus admitted ruefully to himself, enjoyed talking about themselves if their audience was receptive and he was no exception. On the other hand, Miriam Greentree was. The day was proving less successful than he had hoped and one way or another, he wasn't altogether sorry when a glance at his watch followed by a check on the Chinese Crested ring told him March would be free to attend to business.

'We might as well go and find our friend,' he said.

'Why don't you go and find him?' Miriam suggested. 'I'll make my way to the car park and meet you there. You won't want me around while you talk business.'

'We won't be talking business,' Linus told her. 'That's been done. It's simply a matter of picking up the picture and exchanging it for a cheque. Unless I don't like the framing, and that's not very likely.'

'All the same, I'd rather meet you at the car, if you don't mind.'

'You'd bettter have the keys, then,' Linus said, fishing them out of his pocket and dropping them into her hand. 'Are you sure you know which car it is?'

'I'm sure. It's a grey Sierra hatchback and it's in line with the third tree on the left of the red tractor.'

Linus had the unnerving feeling that she could probably have told him the registration number, too, which was more than he could have done, and then he reminded himself that she must have been trained to notice such things so it was hardly surprising. 'Is it?' he said. 'Let's hope no one's moved the tractor, then.'

His way to the benching for toy breeds took him past the veterinary tent and, on an impulse to find out more about Miriam, he stepped inside. Chilson was still on duty, a plastic tumbler of light ale before him.

'Hello,' he said. 'Lost your girlfriend?'

'She's gone back to the car. There was something I meant to ask you. Did the Kennel Club ever take up that suggestion I made?'

'Which suggestion was that?'

'About hiring a private detective.'

'No. I mentioned it in passing, but it was an idea they'd already discarded so nothing more was done, I'm afraid. Did it matter?' He seemed surprised.

'No, not at all—just idle curiosity. Actually, I'd be quite interested to find out what you do discover about our friend. It's all very intriguing.'

'I'll keep you in the picture.' Chilson laughed. 'Sorry. The pun was unintentional.'

'Apology accepted,' replied Linus, who did not regard the pun as the highest form of humour ever invented.

As he ducked out of the doorway of the tent, he was mildly annoyed. He had been so sure, and Miriam had never corrected any of his assumptions. It had suddenly struck him that Chilson would be likely to know the name of Miriam's employers and that through them he might be able to find out more about her. Another good idea bites the dust, he thought bitterly.

He had reached the entrance to the benching tent before the implications of Chilson's words struck him.

If the Kennel Club wasn't directly or indirectly paying Miriam to watch Raymond March, then who was?

And why?

And did it really matter? After all, his own interest in March was hardly personal and it was beginning to look as if a relationship with Miriam was unlikely to develop. Perhaps he'd better stick to business. He pushed aside the flap and went in.

He soon found the number sequence for Chinese Cresteds and then spotted the flush of red cards over the art dealer's benches. 'Well done,' he said. 'Obviously a good day.'

'Not bad. Not bad at all. I must admit I'd have liked Best of Breed but since it was won by something I bred, I'm not complaining too loudly. Shall we go?'

Both men were obviously accompanying him, which surprised Linus: his past experience of dog shows had led him to expect one of them to stay behind with the dogs.

'Will the dogs be all right?' he asked.

'Don't worry, we've arranged for someone to keep an eye on them.'

It occurred to Linus as they made their way to the back of the car park—March must have got there very early to be that far from the gate—that the value of the picture and the combined security of it and his cheque were worth the relatively small risk of leaving the dogs even if someone weren't keeping an eye on them.

Linus had previously guessed that March would take his dogs to shows in a Volvo estate or a Range-Rover. Either would fit the cultivated image, especially when one took the hair and the chain into account. He had guessed wrong. He was taken to a once-white transit which was far from new and hadn't seen a car-wash for a very long time indeed. It was nondescript, dented, not at all what he had expected and there were at least a dozen just like it dotted about the car park.

The discus thrower unlocked the side door and slid them back. Linus saw that the interior had been kitted out for long-distance dog shows. On either side of the opening were banks of cages, while the other side had been fitted up very much like a caravan, with two bunk beds and a small kitchen unit consisting of a sink and a two-ring hob, presumably fuelled by bottled gas. There was a partition cutting the cab off from the rear.

March noticed Linus's surprise. 'Neat, isn't it?' he said. 'Very useful, too. You see, I show all over the UK, and you can't get to Scotland and back to Henley in one day—not if you want to show dogs as well. We prefer to find hotels but it isn't always possible. This solves the problem. Now, to business. You have the cheque?'

Linus took his wallet out of his inside pocket and extracted the banker's draft. March took it, studied it and handed it back.

'That's fine. Now for the picture.'

He took some keys from his pocket and inserted first one, then another, into small keyholes that Linus hadn't noticed and which were in the floor on either side of the opening. He turned them simultaneously and Linus heard the faint 'click' as the lock, or locks, turned.

He became aware that the discus thrower was standing with his back to the transit, taking no interest in what March was doing. His interest was on whether they were being watched and, as far as Linus could tell, the car park was virtually empty.

March put his fingers into a small indentation and pulled. Soundlessly, a false floor, the width of the van's side opening and as long as the transit was wide, slid out. Linus estimated it to be maybe as much as six inches deep. On it, wrapped and loosely tied, lay several pictures. No wonder March hadn't been worried about transporting them with the dogs. He removed the largest of them and pushed the false floor back straight away. Linus heard the locks click into place. He and March became simply two men looking at a painting. Linus recalled Chilson's comment about falling off the back of a lorry and his unease returned.

March unwrapped the picture. 'Well?' he said.

It had been well done. Neither the mount nor the frame could have been bettered.

'Perfect,' Linus told him.

'Good.' March began to re-wrap the picture, more securely this time.

'There is just one thing,' Linus said. 'I should have asked before, I suppose.'

'Yes?' March sounded wary. That might be because there was something wrong or it might be because he was afraid Linus was going to back out of the deal.

'Provenance. Does it come with a pedigree?'

'Incomplete. Two previous bills of sale, both recent. One to me and one to the previous owner, though that has a note from the seller detailing the tradition within the family as to how and when it came into their possession. I haven't been able to authenticate that, I'm afraid, so it's nothing more than curiosity value.'

'But you've no doubts about it?'

'None at all. Why? Have you?'

'I'm not sufficiently knowledgeable. I have to leave it to you, but I'd hate someone to come along in a few years' time and lay claim to it. Remember, by my standards it's a lot of money.'

'Point taken. You can rest easy on that score.' March accepted Linus's draft and handed him an envelope in return. 'It's all there and if you've any further doubts, well, you know where to find me. I've been there a long time and I don't anticipate moving.'

All in all, Linus felt a bit of a fool though he knew he had been no such thing—except, perhaps, in so far as he had left the important matter of provenance until the eleventh hour.

He made his way back to the car. Miriam was already in the passenger seat but she'd had the commonsense to open all the doors and windows to let some air in. The day hadn't been exceptionally hot but the insides of cars heat up very quickly.

Linus had thrown an old candlewick bedspread and a short length of carpet into the back of the car before he had left home. Now he laid the carpet carefully on the floor of the boot, making quite sure there was no unevenness underneath it. He placed his picture on this and covered the whole with thc bcdsprcad, wrong side uppermost. His boots, tow-rope, took-kit and oilcan he placed on the back seat.

Miriam watched him, frowning. 'Wouldn't it be better to put the picture on the seat?' she asked.

Linus looked shocked. 'And have it shoot forward if I have to brake suddenly? It's safer on a completely flat surface that it can't fall off.'

It was still only the middle of the afternoon when they arrived back at the service area where Miriam had left her car. She glanced at her watch. 'Shall we have a cup of tea?' she suggested.

Linus glanced behind him and sighed. 'I could do with one but I'm not leaving this little lot unattended.' He hesitated. 'I don't suppose you'd like to round the day off with dinner?'

'Fine. Where shall we meet?'

Linus mentioned a restaurant in the city and then chuckled. 'Of course, if I had a vehicle like March's, we could have that cup of tea quite safely.'

She smiled. 'I saw you go over to that very run-down looking van. You're right. No one would expect there to be anything of value in that.'

'That's not the reason,' Linus told her. 'The whole vehicle's fitted out, not just for dog shows, but for transporting pictures.'

'But how? I'd have thought the two were mutually exclusive.'

'Not the way he does it. There's a very cleverly concealed false bottom to that transit. It's a sort of drawer that must be nearly six inches deep. It locks by means of keyholes on the inside and when it's closed, you simply wouldn't know it was there. Very clever.'

'But rather secretive.'

'True. On the other hand, it's as safe as Securicor and a lot more unobtrusive. Remember, I bought one of his cheaper pictures. It would be a good way of transporting much more valuable ones as well as the stuff he sells at shows.'

'I wonder how often he sells a good one?' Miriam speculated.

'At his sort of price, you don't have to move many pictures in a year to do very nicely indeed.'

Either Miriam was less than fascinated by the subject under discussion or she was desperate for a cup of tea. Whatever the reason, she cut the conversation short by opening the car door and getting out. She smiled in at Linus. 'I'll see you this evening, then,' she said before closing it and crossing to her own car.

Linus turned the key and watched her in the mirror. Perhaps another opportunity to follow her was about to present itself. In daylight, too, which would be easier. He saw her pause by her car. Then she turned and headed towards the café. The cup of tea had won and an opportunity had slipped by.

Linus was conscious of a quite irrational sense of disappointment. Something whispered to him that this relationship—if, indeed, it could be dignified by such a word—was doomed. Perhaps it had been silly to make a date for this evening. Perhaps it would have been better to let it simply die. It certainly wasn't going anywhere at any great rate of knots. So why didn't he just let go? Because I'm middle-aged and ordinary, and women like Miriam

Greentree don't come my way very often. That's why, he told himself. And there's always the chance that this time it'll work out.

CHAPTER 5

The evening was not a great success and Linus would have been the first to admit that this was largely his fault. He could not leave well alone. The lack of personal information which Miriam was prepared to release not only irritated him but made him much more curious than he would otherwise have been. He was unsure whether what he really wanted to know was more about her private life, or her reason for taking such an interest in March; and although Chilson had told him the Kennel Club had nothing to do with it, he used that as his starting point, partly because she had never disabused him of the idea. Since none of his oblique approaches had worked, he'd better try the direct attack.

'Will you satisfy my curiosity on one thing?' he asked.

She was instantly wary. 'If I can, but I don't guarantee it.'

'Your interest in March. Have you been hired by the Kennel Club?'

'No.'

The answer was blunt and if Linus had hoped it would be followed by the real reason, he was disappointed.

'You must have known I thought they were behind it. Why didn't you put me right before?'

'It didn't seem important. Why should they be interested?'

'Something to do with his age,' Linus said, making it sound vague. 'There's an idea he's older than he says.'

'What does he say?'

'Sixty-five.'

'What would you put him at?'

'He could be that, I suppose, but I'd add at least three, possibly five more years.'

She nodded. 'That would make more sense.' She pushed her fettucini around the plate as if she were uncertain whether to drop the subject and thereby silence Linus's curiosity or whether to find out more to satisfy her own. 'Why does his age matter?' she asked.

'I gather it's a question of whether he's eligible for some committee or other. One or two people think he's had cosmetic surgery.'

'Do you?'

'It didn't cross my mind until after someone had mentioned it. Then I could see their point but I'm hardly a qualified opinion.'

'You're not a member of the Kennel Club, either, are you?'

'No.' Linus wondered why she'd bothered to find out. 'Is that relevant?'

'I wondered why they should have discussed it with you at all.'

'It wasn't "discussed". Someone who knew I'd met him aksed my opinion, that's all.' It was near enough to the truth not to be an outright lie.

It seemed to satisfy Miriam and she turned the conversation effortlessly into an unconnected channel without the join being apparent. It was only as Linus toyed with a fresh fruit salad that he realized his attempts at eliciting information had been neatly turned back on him and Miriam had discovered a great deal while he had discovered only what Chilson had already told him. Nothing he had told Miriam came into the category of State Secrets any more than did the information he had hoped to glean from her, but it was unnerving to find she was so much better at it than he.

Coffee was a tiny cup of froth and Linus looked at it with distaste. Apart from anything else, he knew from experience that it was impossible to drink it without the froth sticking to the neatly trimmed hair of his beard and moustache and he could never be quite sure he had wiped it all off when he'd finished.

Miriam saw his distaste. 'You don't live far from here, do you?' she said. 'Why don't we go back there for some proper coffee?'

It was just about the last suggestion he expected her to make. He grinned. 'Good idea. I wish I'd suggested it myself.'

He let them both in to the small artisan's cottage and went on through to the kitchen to start the coffee. His new picture was propped up on an armchair while he decided where it should hang. In view of the fact that it was the sole reason they had trekked over to the dog show, he would have expected her to show at least a polite interest in it, but there was none just as, on her previous visit, she hadn't appeared even to notice what was on the walls.

He drew her attention to it. 'This is it,' he said.

She seemed a little startled, as if her thoughts had been elsewhere. 'It?' she repeated. 'Oh, your new picture.' She glanced at it. 'Cows,' she said, stating the obvious. 'I'm glad you're happy with it but I can't say it would have been my first choice for subject matter.'

'Nor mine,' Linus agreed. 'It's just that he's handled it so well.' He hesitated. 'I don't suppose you'd like to suggest where it ought to be hung?'

It obviously wasn't something to which she'd given any thought at all and she looked round the room indecisively. 'What about there?' she said, indicating a wall opposite the window. 'I should think it would fit in quite well beside that little landscape.'

Linus shook his head. 'It's a watercolour. That means it mustn't be hung in direct sunlight. They fade.'

Miriam laughed. 'I'm not very good at this. I'm sure you'll find the right place for it.'

Linus knew he would. It might take a day or two, maybe as long as a week, and he would probably have to move something else, but he had little doubt that the right spot would occur to him quite suddenly, out of the blue. It often happened that way.

He brought the coffee into the sitting-room, decent sized cups neatly arranged on the tray, and tried not to read too much into the fact that Miriam had chosen to sit in the other armchair, thus effectively depriving him of the chance of sitting next to her. He perched on the sofa and poured.

'Are you quite happy about that picture?' Miriam asked him suddenly as he handed her a cup.

'I wish it hadn't cost quite so much but apart from that, yes, why shouldn't I be?'

'I was thinking about what your friend said—about it's having fallen off the back of a lorry.'

'Not impossible, but not very likely,' Linus told her. 'I've got some provenance—bills of sale covering the last two owners.'

'Isn't it older than that?'

'Quite a bit and I can't deny there might have been some hanky-panky at some time in its past but March seems satisfied and he is, after all, a dealer of some repute.'

'Can't things like bills of sale be forged?'

'Anything can be forged but frankly, I don't think this is an important enough picture to make it worth the effort.'

'You don't, for example, think it could be . . . oh, I don't know . . . something stolen during the war and been hidden for forty-five years until everyone's forgotten about it and then released on to the market?'

Linus stared at her for a moment and then laughed. 'We're not talking Rembrandt here,' he said. 'Ten years and a change of country would be all this would have needed before it resurfaced.'

'Not all the pictures the Nazis secreted can have been great masterpieces.'

'True, and it's precisely the lesser ones like this that could finance the thieves while they waited until it was safe to sell off the good ones.'

'So maybe that's why it has only limited provenance,' Miriam pointed out.

Linus looked at her. Miriam's demeanour was that of someone conducting a purely academic argument but he thought there was more to it than that. She was right, though the probability was remote. From time to time pictures *did* surface which were alleged to be part of Goering's private collection, or some such nonsense—in fact, hadn't he been reading about one such case fairly recently? He tried to remember the details but couldn't. It didn't much matter. The stories usually petered out into nothing and more often than not the pictures concerned turned out to be very clever forgeries snapped up by some greedy and none too scrupulous collector who eventually had to boast of what he'd acquired and was then discovered to have been bad.

Linus's eyes narrowed slightly. She wasn't just tossing ideas around and he didn't think she was trying to upset him. 'Exactly what *is* your interest in March?' he asked.

The question was followed by silence. Linus had the impression she hadn't expected quite so direct a question. He wondered how evasive her answer would be.

'You don't beat about the bush, do you?' she said.

'Not as much as you do. Well?'

Miriam moved uneasily in her chair. 'Improbable as it may seem, I'm part of a small international band of people who are trying to track down some of the missing works of art. There's probably not as many still in existence as the popular press would have everyone believe, but there are some, and we're reasonably sure March was actively involved in their theft when he was in the SS as a young man. Our first concern is to trace as many of the pictures as we can. When we're satisfied that we can't track any more through this particular source, we'll see whether he can't be brought to trial.'

'Rubbish,' Linus said flatly.

'Do you deny the stories that there was a Nazi haul of works of art?'

'No. No, that seems to be well enough documented.'

'So why do you say it's rubbish?'

Linus thought about it. 'Partly because it's just too far-fetched, too melodramatic to be probable.'

'Don't they say truth is stranger than fiction?'

Linus had to concede that it very often was. 'But this is illogical,' he went on.

'How?'

'Let's assume your basic premise is right, and March had a hand in stealing all these masterpieces. Let's assume he had a hand in hiding them, which is possible, though if I'd been masterminding something along those lines, I'd have made jolly sure the people doing the actual hiding wouldn't know what was being hidden. Still, if we allow for the chaos of the last weeks of the war, maybe the planning was a bit rushed. March knows what's been stolen and he knows where it's been hidden. Sooner or later he sets about filtering some of these masterpieces on to the market, thereby making himself a very rich man. Have I got it right?'

'I couldn't have explained it better myself,' Miriam told him.

'In the circumstances, don't you think it was a bit daft to become an art dealer himself? I mean, once there was a hint of doubt about one piece and it was traced back to him, his connection would be obvious.'

The quiet smile on Miriam's face faded. 'If he wasn't an art dealer, how else could he do it?'

'By taking someone else into his confidence and setting them up to do the selling. Oh, it would be risky, especially if they fell out, but I think there'd be enough money involved to guarantee a good working partnership.'

'On the other hand, the very fact that it was too obvious would be inclined to make people look further than March himself, don't you think?'

Linus shrugged. 'Bluff and counter-bluff. I'm not a poker-player. I don't know which is the more likely. I just think the whole thing's too far-fetched. Chilson might have something when he says the picture probably fell off the back of a lorry. There are plenty of country-house art thefts these days so that's much more likely. I hope not because I'm not sure where that would leave me, but I feel bound to say that while I can't pretend I like March very much, I have a feeling that so far as his merchandise is concerned, he's an honest man.'

Miriam put her cup on the table. 'What you choose to believe is entirely your privilege,' she said. 'You asked me and I told you. The rest's up to you.' She glanced at her watch. 'Goodness, is that the time?' She stood up. 'It's been a lovely evening, Linus—a super meal and an interesting discussion but I really must go.'

He stood up and helped her into her jacket. 'And I've got an early start in the morning,' he said. 'What about dinner later in the week? We'll stick to less contentious issues.'

She laughed. 'Thursday? Let's go to the Mitre, like the tourists.'

'The Mitre it is.' He opened the door and watched until she was safely in her car before closing it again.

Somewhat to his surprise, he wasn't the least bit depressed that she had so clearly not wished the evening to culminate in a greater degree of closeness. That something along those lines was what she had had in mind when she suggested coming back to Osney Mead had been a very welcome thought at the time, so why wasn't he downhearted that it hadn't happened? A woman who didn't tell you anything about herself was intriguing and eventually, annoying. One who lied was something else.

For someone who was tracking down lost masterpieces, Miriam Greentree was quite remarkably ignorant about the whole subject.

Linus arrived at the Mitre some twenty minutes before the time he and Miriam had agreed on. He always made a point of being a little early because he remembered how his wife hated to have to wait alone for him. She told him she always felt vulnerable and that all too many of the men who approached with an 'All on your own tonight, love?' were unpleasantly reluctant to believe 'No.' Ever since then, he had seen to it that no woman ever had to wait for him if they were meeting in a public place. At the very least he would telephone wherever it was and explain that he had been delayed.

On this occasion it wouldn't have mattered very much if he had been late. Miriam didn't arrive.

Linus gave her half an hour and debted whether to go home again but then he decided that since he was here, he might as well enjoy it so he ordered a steak and was forced to admit to himself when he'd finished that he'd scarcely noticed Miriam's absence. She was a good-looking woman, the sort a man was pleased to be seen out with, but he had already begun to realize that there was unlikely ever to be more to it than that. They had very little in common and although Linus thought he moved quite easily between town and country, she not only had no experience of the latter, but no interest, either. To her 'the country' was a land as foreign as Japan. More so, probably: he guessed she'd be quite at home among the luxury shops of Tokyo. What's more, he didn't think she had ever been under quite the same degree of romantic illusion as he.

Well, he'd got the message and it wasn't unpalatable. It was probably just as well that he didn't have a number or an address at which he could contact her, even if he wanted to, and she was unlikely to contact him after standing him up.

And if she did? Linus's self-confidence, limited where women were concerned, had to admit the possibility. He considered it dispassionately. If she did, he thought he would prove to be up to his ears in work. There was very little point in anything else.

When he left the Mitre, he was in a perfectly tranquil frame of mind.

Linus finally decided on the right place for his newly-acquired cow. At least three other pictures had to be juggled around before he was satisfied with it but at last everything was in an appropriate place and he made himself some coffee and sat on his bed, propping himself up with the pillows as if he were an invalid, to drink the coffee and admire the picture. It was on a blank wall that had once been a chimney-breast and those lovely, tender eyes would be the first thing he saw in the morning and the last thing he saw at night, which couldn't be bad.

He had heard nothing more from Miriam and was quite pleased that his self-esteem didn't even feel dented. He went back over her extraordinary claim that March was an ex-Nazi and wondered whether one could ever be truly 'ex' in that context. Then there was her bizarre claim that he was gradually releasing on to the market the pictures stolen by his confederates during the war. For 'market' read 'private market', he thought. Nothing that was well documented before the war could possibly appear on the open market without being spotted. Well, there was no doubt a lot of things had been stolen and had disappeared apparently without trace. From what little he had read about it, there were people who devoted their spare time to trying to discover where one such hoard was hidden, rather as there were people who tried to track down gold-laden galleons in the Caribbean or, for that matter, the Loch Ness Monster. They were latter-day treasure-seekers for whom the travelling was at least as satisfying as an arrival would be: there had to be a goal worth attaining but it didn't much matter if it remained elusive.

From time to time something emerged which was said to come from such a hoard. There had been an instance in the paper only a few weeks ago. Whether or not that proved to be its source, it had the same effect as someone finding a dubloon, or a new photo purporting to be the Monster: it spurred others on with renewed optimism.

He found it hard to believe that he should have stumbled across it. Harder still to believe that someone who knew nothing at all about pictures or even how to hang them should be part of a team tracking them down. Besides, he remembered suddenly, the problem with March was that his background was untraceable. No, whatever Miriam's reason for watching March might be, it wasn't that.

Linus grinned to himself. He had an idea. He swung his feet off the bed and went downstairs with his mug. Brought up to be punctilious—'Don't put it down, put it away'—he washed it under the tap, dried it and put it back in the cupboard. Then he picked up the telephone.

'Chilson, have you got a minute? Good. Listen, let me throw this one at you in relation to your friend March.'

'You mean you've found something out? Go on.'

'Would you believe he was born in Germany?'

There was a pause. 'No accent,' Chilson objected.

'Doesn't have to be. Look at Robert Maxwell—born in Czechoslovakia and he didn't have one either. What's more *he* didn't sound as if he'd had elocution lessons, and March does.'

There was another pause. 'OK. I'll buy that.'

'As a young man he was responsible either for stealing or for hiding—and quite possibly both—some of the art treasures which now he's in an ideal position to ease on to the market and pick up a fortune.'

'Wouldn't he be a rather obvious suspect?'

'Plastic surgery to change his appearance, and in particular make him look too young to have been involved? Forged papers? I bet if your people ask him to produce a birth certificate, he'd produce a German one—forged, but the Kennel Club wouldn't be in a position to spot that—stating he was the age he said he was.'

Another pause followed this exposition. 'I'll tell you what I think, Rintoul. I think you've been hitting the bottle. Either that or you've been out in the sun too long, but since this is England I'll put my money on the bottle.'

Linus laughed, unoffended. 'I found it hard to swallow, too.'

'You mean someone put this forward in all seriousness?'

'That's right. The woman I was at Bath with.'

'She didn't strike me as the least bit barmy. You'd better watch yourself there, old man.'

'Nothing to watch. It petered out.'

'Just as well, if that's the sort of ideas she came up with. Any objection if I get on with some work?'

Linus put the phone down. There were times when the opinion of a sane friend was just what one needed.

*

'Mr Rintoul? Mr Linus Rintoul?' There were two men on the doorstep and the speaker was sharp-faced and a sharp dresser. His companion was neither and Linus had seen them both before though he couldn't place them immediately.

The speaker produced his warrant card and held it up too briefly for Linus to be able to read it. 'Detective-Inspector Netley and this is Detective-Sergeant Cote. May we come in?'

Linus opened the door and ushered them into the sitting-room. He had met the couple a year or two back at the height of the BSE scare and hadn't warmed to the senior of the two. 'There's a veterinary problem, Detective-Inspector?' he asked.

'Are you aware of one we should know about?'

Linus sighed. He had forgotten the infuriating police propensity for answering one question with another and for reading a confession of guilt into the most innocuous remarks.

'No, Detective-Inspector, but I'm a government vet. There are a number of situations in which you might well require my services. I gather this isn't one of them.'

'May we sit down, Mr Rintoul? We do anticipate being here for quite a while.'

'Be my guest,' Linus told him. It was an Americanism he loathed and it gave him a perverse pleasure to direct it at someone he instinctively disliked. He considered—and rejected—the idea of offering them tea or coffee. The inference of such hospitality would be either that they were welcome, which the Detective-Inspector was not, though Linus had no views on his assistant, or that he was trying to curry favour. Netley would make the latter assumption. So no refreshment.

They each took a chair, leaving Linus with the sofa, and

the Detective-Sergeant took his notebook and pen unobtrusively from his pocket.

Netley had a notebook out, too, but it was to refer to rather than to write in.

'Tell me, Mr Rintoul,' he began. 'Where were you last—' he looked at his notes although Linus was quite sure his memory needed no refreshing—'Thursday?'

'Last Thursday? At work, of course.'

'At work. Does that mean at Government Buildings?'

'That's where MAFF offices are,' Linus pointed out.

'Indeed, but my understanding is that you don't spend all day in the office. Or was this an exception?'

When faced with the Netleys of this world, Linus tended to take refuge in pedantic precision. It irked him to be hoist with his own petard but one had to be fair. 'You're right, of course.'

'So what exactly did you do that day?' Netley persisted.

'My week's records are at the office. They give a blow by blow account, including my times of arrival and leaving.'

'We can look at those later. Right now I'd like to rely on your memory.'

Linus judged this was not a situation in which to admit, however truthfully, to an erratic memory. He was very tempted to ask what this was all about but he knew it would be pointless. If they didn't want him to know just yet, they wouldn't tell him, and when they did think it would serve their purpose by telling him, then they'd do so.

'Thursday,' he said. 'I'll have to go through the day from the beginning—to get the sequence.'

'Couldn't be better.'

'Thursday.' He cast his mind back. 'That was a stockyard day. I didn't go into the office at all to start with. I went straight to Banbury.'

'Do you mean straight to the stockyard or did you stop off anywhere else—to buy a paper, for example?'

'No, straight there.'

'What time did you arrive?'

'You'd have to look at the record to know exactly but it will have been somewhere between eight and eight-thirty.'

'Isn't that a bit early?'

'Not if you want to watch beasts being unloaded. That's when you spot some of the unfit animals. I was there for most of the morning.'

'Can anyone vouch for that?'

'That I was there at all, do you mean? Or that I was there all morning?'

'Both.'

'Yes and no respectively. There was a pig and a couple of sheep I wasn't happy about. The carriers will remember that all right because they argued the toss—as they always do. No one will know I was there all morning because the nature of the job is that you're always moving about. For what it's worth, I had lunch in the pub there. They know me well enough and so do the stockmen who use it. I left the stockyards after I'd eaten.'

'And in the afternoon?'

'We'd had a couple of complaints about sheep that had been left in a field with contaminated water—a pond that the locals had been dumping waste in. That was over Buckingham way. I went to have a look. The pond was contaminated, all right, but they had troughs of fresh water at the top of the field.'

'So no one saw you or spoke to you during that trip?'

Linus grinned. 'I wouldn't say that. The farmer was, well, elusive. They don't always welcome the Man from the Ministry, you know. I eventually winkled him and his sons out of their kitchen.'

'Why did you need to do that if there wasn't a problem? Why not just go once you'd satisfied yourself the sheep were all right?'

'For one thing, I'd been tramping across his land uninvited. You can't do that, you know. Well,' he amended hastily, '*you* probably can. Government vets can't. So I had to make sure he knew about it, keeping it all open and above board. I needed to tell him about the complaint, too. It wasn't justified in so far as the sheep had plenty of good water, but the pond *was* contaminated and I warned him he'd better fence it off. The fences had been broken down on the field side.'

'And he'll verify all this?'

'I imagine so, though he'll be even more reluctant to talk to you than he was to me.' Linus glanced at the Detective-Sergeant. 'In fact, I'd suggest your assistant would be more successful in dealing with him.'

It was the wrong thing to say, and Netley bristled. 'And why would you think that?'

'I wasn't trying to be offensive, Detective-Inspector. Your sergeant is a countryman born and bred. Some countryfolk are a breed apart and the direct, sharp approach isn't necessarily the right one to use. Your sergeant will know exactly how to lead up to what he wants to know. It'll take time but I'll lay you any odds you like he'll draw more out of them than you will.'

Both men glanced at the Detective-Sergeant and Linus thought he saw the hint of a small smile. His superior didn't press the matter.

'What then?' he asked.

'Then I *did* go back to the office. Partly to let them know I was still in the land of the living and partly to check whether there had been any calls for me.'

'Did you have any reason to expect any?'

Linus thought the man's interest had sharpened. 'Not really. Today's calls often decide tomorrow's programme, so one checks. It did cross my mind that there might be one cancelling an arrangement I'd made for the evening.'

'And was there?'

The sharpened interest wasn't an illusion, Linus decided. 'No,' he said.

'So tell me about this . . . arrangement.'

'It was a date. With a woman.'

'Her name?'

Linus told him.

'And where were you to meet?'

'At the Mitre. At half-past seven.' Linus volunteered the time because it was obviously going to be the next question.

'Did you keep the appointment?'

'I did. She didn't.'

'She didn't get tired of waiting for you and go home?'

'Hardly, Detective-Inspector. I was a good twenty minutes early and I waited until about eight.'

'Then you went home?'

'No. I was going to but then I thought since I was there I might as well have something to eat, so I had a steak and a glass of wine and *then* I went home.'

'What time would this be?'

'I can't be sure. The service wasn't all that fast and I didn't hurry over it, either. At a guess I'd say after half past nine and before ten.'

'You can't be any more precise than that?'

'No, I can't. As a matter of fact, I can't even be *that* precise. If someone swears blind I left at nine-fifteen or at ten-fifteen, I couldn't swear otherwise. Though I'd be a bit surprised,' he added as an afterthought.

'Let's be quite sure I understand you,' Netley said. 'You're telling me that this—' he appeared to check his notes again. '—this Miriam Greentree didn't keep the date.'

'That's right.'

'But you did?'

'I've just told you so.'

'And the staff at the Mitre will be able to vouch for your presence there?'

'I certainly hope so.'

Netley looked at him through narrowed eyes. 'Now why should you be so emphatic about hoping they do? Does it worry you that they might not?'

Linus took a deep breath. This was not the time for the facetious answer. 'Because, Detective-Inspector, I'm not stupid enough to imagine you've come here because you've nothing better to do with your time. You're a detective. You arrive on my doorstep with your sergeant, flashing your IDs and asking a lot of questions. I haven't the foggiest idea what those questions are all about, but I don't doubt at all that you've a very good reason for asking them, and if somebody's done something and my name has come up, and my being able to prove I was at the Mitre exonerates me from whatever it is, then, yes, I certainly hope the staff remember me. Does that sound reasonable?'

Netley permitted himself a small, thin-lipped smile. 'Eminently, Mr Rintoul. You don't think there will be a problem?'

'There shouldn't be. I suppose it depends to some extent upon their memories. And Access, of course.'

'Access? I'm not sure I follow.'

'I paid for my meal with Access. It doesn't help with the time, I suppose, but at least it proves I was there.'

The fact was duly noted. 'Had you seen Miss Greentree at any time during the day?'

'No.'

'And what did you do after your dinner?'

'I told you—I went home.'

'That's right, so you did. Tell me, did you go straight home?'

'Yes.'

'You didn't by any chance make a little detour to find

out why Miss Greentree had stood you up? To see whether she was ill, or something?'

Linus smiled ruefully. 'I couldn't have done that if I'd wanted to. I don't know where she lives.'

The policeman was polite but incredulous. 'What do you mean—you don't know where she lives?'

'I mean exactly that. I don't even know whether she lives in the city or in one of the surrounding towns. For all I know, she may live in London and commute. I haven't a clue.'

'Was this your first date, then?'

'No, we've been out together several times.'

'Are you expecting us to believe that you've never taken her home?'

'I've no control over what you believe, Detective-Inspector,' Linus said tetchily. 'The fact remains that I didn't. She'd been back here a couple of times but we always met at whichever restaurant we'd decided on, and except for those two occasions, she always drove straight home from there.'

'And is that what she did last Thursday?'

'I've already told you, I didn't see her on Thursday. As you so aptly expressed it yourself, she stood me up.'

'So you must have been quite annoyed by the time you got home. You couldn't drop in on her and demand an explanation because you didn't know where she lived, so presumably as soon as you got indoors you telephoned her.'

Linus was finding it hard to remain patient but he made the effort because he suspected that at least part of Netley's purpose was to wind him up so that he would say something injudicious upon which the detective could pounce. 'I didn't ring her, either, and for exactly the same reason: I don't know her number.'

'You went out several times with an attractive woman without finding out her address or her phone number?

Doesn't that strike you as a very strange sort of relationship?'

'Yes, it does. Except that it didn't really merit the word "relationship". It was too loose for that—and I don't use the word in its moral sense.'

'And you had no curiosity about it at all?'

'I was curious, yes. I did try to find out her phone number—her name's not in the book but there could be several reasons for that. They wouldn't give a number, or even say if there was one, unless I could give them the address which, of course, I couldn't. I tried to follow her one evening but I lost her. In any case, it seemed a sneaky thing to do and, besides, there wasn't ever another opportunity.'

All this was duly written down and then Netley closed his notebook. 'Do you know what strikes me as very, very odd about this whole interview, Mr Rintoul?' he asked.

'No, but I've a feeling you may be going to tell me.'

'It's the fact that not once have you asked what it's all about. Now that suggests one of two things to me, Mr Rintoul. Either you are one of the most incurious people in Britain, or you already know. Which is it?'

Linus laughed. 'Neither. I haven't a clue what it's all about and I'm as curious as the next man but, in my limited dealings with the police, I've learnt that you won't tell me until it suits you to do so, and when that time comes you'll tell me without my having to ask.'

Netley studied him for a few minutes as if he were trying to discover some Machiavellian purpose behind the answer. 'Then I can only congratulate you on your restraint,' he said and Linus had the impression he meant it. 'What do you know about Miss Greentree?'

Linus glanced across at the sergeant and noticed that his notebook had never been closed. The interview wasn't over yet. 'Next to nothing,' he said. 'She wasn't only reticent about her address and telephone number. She never, at any time, said anything at all about her family, her home, her education. Nothing. She was able to sustain an interesting conversation without going into any personal details at all. I've no idea what her politics were, or her religion, or her taste in music or books. I do know she wasn't a vegetarian, for what that's worth. But that's it. No, I lie. I learnt one thing.'

The pen was poised. 'What was that, Mr Rintoul?'

'She used to collect stamps when she was a child.'

'Are you trying to be funny?' Netley asked suspiciously.

'Not at all. That was the only piece of information she ever let slip.'

'Doesn't that strike you as rather odd?'

'Lots of children collect stamps.' A glance at Netley's face told him that the comment was not appreciated. 'Yes, Detective-Inspector, it did strike as rather odd but there wasn't much I could do about it.'

'Has she been in touch since she stood you up?'

'No.'

'Does that upset you?'

'No. I enjoyed her company but as far as I could make out, we didn't share any common ground at all. I suppose, in a way, I wasn't altogether surprised that she didn't turn up, and when I thought about it I decided it was probably the easiest and most painless way there was to end the acquaintance.'

'And you can't throw any more light on her at all?'

Linus thought of her story about the Nazi looters and their hidden hoard of treasure but he wasn't about to pass that load of old cobblers on to a man like Netley. If he did, the man would think he was a candidate for certification, either for making it up himself, or for having taken it seriously enough to repeat.

'No, none,' he said. 'But I would like to know what this is all about.'

Another of Netley's thin smiles flitted across his sharp features. 'I think we've reached a stage where you can be told, Mr Rintoul,' he said. 'At some time on Thursday evening—certainly before nine o'clock—Miss Greentree was murdered.'

The colour drained out of Linus's face and the normally pale scars hidden by his neatly-trimmed beard stood out livid by contrast. 'Murdered?' he said. 'You don't just mean dead?'

'Murdered.'

'But how? By whom?'

'If we knew who did it, we wouldn't he here. As for how, I'm afraid there's no problem about that. Her neck was broken by a blow possibly from something along the lines of a baseball bat and then, to make things absolutely sure, her skull was battered in. It wasn't subtle, it wasn't suicide, and she wasn't recognizable.'

Linus shuddered. He felt suddenly sick. 'That's . . . horrible,' he said, deeply conscious of the inadequacy of the word. 'And in one's own home where one would feel safe.'

'It wasn't very nice,' the detective agreed laconically. 'But why do you assume it was in her own home?'

'I don't know . . . I suppose I thought . . .' Linus looked at him. 'Wasn't it?'

'Nowhere near. It was in Portsmouth, on a deserted sort of pier called the Square Tower. Do you know it?'

Linus shook his head. 'I've been there—Portsmouth, I mean—but I can't claim to know it. What was she doing there?'

'That's what we'd like to know. It's taken a long time just to identify her. Your phone number—both your phone numbers—were in her diary along with a note of Thursday's date, but it had been crossed out. We're checking back through every contact we can find, however remote. We'll be checking your statements, of course, but it looks as if you'd have had a job to be in Portsmouth, and we're satisfied she was killed there and not elsewhere and dumped. In the meantime, I suggest you have a stiff drink. And if anything comes back to you that you think might be useful, you'll get in touch, won't you?'

'Yes. Yes, of course.'

The two policemen let themselves out of the house, but Linus was hardly aware of their going. He sat stunned for several minutes and it took the sound of Ishmael scratching at the back door to be let in, to bring him back to his surroundings.

He let the dog in and then poured himself a measure of malt, hesitated, and doubled it. Then he sat down with the glass in one hand and absent-mindedly put the other round the dog's neck. Ishmael had sensed that things were different today and that he could sit on the sofa beside Linus with impunity for once. His instincts were right. There were occasions when the silent, uncritical, unquestioning companionship of a dog is what a person needs.

CHAPTER 6

The whisky and the dog provided only temporary relief from the horrors of Miriam's death. Linus still found it hard to believe, in the way that news of any unexpected death is always hard to believe but, in addition to that, he felt as guilty as if he had killed her himself. He was perfectly well aware that guilt was an entirely illogical emotion in the circumstances. In the first place, there was the very simple fact that he hadn't done it. He hadn't even been there to prevent someone else doing it, yet his was precisely where his guilt lay, or so it seemed to him. If he had been with her, he might have been able to prevent it, and he should have been with her—they had had a date, after all. The fact that she was killed in a city some ninety miles from their rendezvous and that she hadn't kept the date anyway, did little to assuage his feeling of guilt. Neither did the fact that, if she had crossed through the assignation in her diary it suggested she had decided some time previously not to keep it and that it was therefore not a matter of chance that she had been elsewhere.

Linus reproached himself with not having made a more determined effort to find out where she lived, with not having insisted on having a phone number so that he could contact her. Netley was right: it wasn't natural to be so incurious. If he had made that extra effort, if he had insisted on a number, at least he could have phoned to find out if she were all right. Common sense told him that, by the time he had done so, she might well already have been dead and must certainly have been in Portsmouth by then, so his call couldn't possibly have made one iota of difference. All the same, he felt he had not proved a very good friend and the fact that around the time he was deciding it was a friendship with no future, she must have been lying in a pool of blood on a deserted pier, made him feel not only guilty but also treacherous, as if he had in some way betrayed her.

The news of her brutal death shook him more than he liked to admit, and when he awoke next day after a night broken by nightmare visions and imagined screams, he decided he couldn't face the normality of the office and usual routine, so he rang in sick even though he guessed that the best cure for this particular brand of depression might be to immerse himself in work.

He was making a very good attempt to immerse himself in whisky when two thoughts occurred to him, admittedly a little blurred around the edges. The first was that if he was drinking to drown his sorrows, he might as well drink meths, since this was a complete waste of a very fine malt; the second was that some useful purpose might be served by his going to see where she died. He had no idea what. So far as clues to her murderer's identity were concerned, the police were far and away the best people to solve that particular puzzle. He suspected that the reason was actually a great deal more primitive than that. In order to accept a death, contact with that death needed to be quite close. If one could not be with the sufferer at the moment of death, it helped to at least see the body, which was why, in Linus's youth, neighbours and friends had visited those who had died and who were laid out in the front parlour for that purpose. This wasn't feasible in Miriam's case and a visit to the place where she died was the next best thing. When he stopped to think logically, without the intrusion of guilt and sorrow, he couldn't honestly conceive of any other useful purpose that might be served by his going to Portsmouth, but if it eased his grief and guilt then that was surely justification enough.

He couldn't go today. He felt unnaturally sober but he had enough sense to realize that he couldn't be and he was certainly well over the driving limit. He put what was left of the whisky firmly back in its cupboard and made himself some very strong black coffee. After that he had some lunch and did some quick calculations. Today was Wednesday. He could take Thursday and Friday off without needing a doctor's certificate. He picked up the telephone, took a deep breath and lied convincingly.

The simple fact that he was doing something did much to raise Linus's spirits as he headed south across the Vale of Oxford and over the rolling downs, lushly green in their winter wheat. He eschewed the motorway into Portsmouth, preferring the visual excitement of cresting the last and most westerly outcrop of the South Downs to see the island city laid out beneath him. The tide was in and the sun shimmered silver grey on the water. It was more than beautiful; it was magical, as magical as—he plundered a life's experiences to find a worthy comparison—as the moving, shimmering silver of semen under a microscope. He smiled at the comparison. It was a just one, but if Miriam had been offended by his mention of muddy udders, what would she have made of that? He chuckled and then felt guilty. Levity should have no place in the mourning process unless, perhaps, it was an indication that he was already beginning to come to terms with her death, if not with the manner of it. He didn't think he could ever come to terms with that.

He got back in his car and drove slowly along the crest of the hill, reluctant to lose, even temporarily, that view of the sea. Born in Bristol himself, the sea always exerted a pull which was more than mere nostalgia. Its presence affected the light and the air, and whenever Linus returned to Oxford after a visit to any part of the coast, both the city and its surrounding hills—the Cotswolds to the west and the Chilterns to the east—were unbearably claustrophobic for the first few days after his return. Conversely, when he smelled sea air again after an interval away, he felt refreshed and invigorated.

He drove into Old Portsmouth and booked in at the Dolphin where he had stayed once before. His recollection of the city's layout was vague, but he thought the Square Tower was quite close. When he asked the receptionist, she regarded him with closer interest.

'The Square Tower? Turn left outside the door and it's straight in front of you. Are you a reporter?'

'No, a vet.' His surprise was unfeigned.

'We've had quite a lot of them over the last few days. A

woman was murdered there. You might have read about it.' She shuddered with the horrified delight possible only in someone with a limited imagination and leant confidingly across the desk. 'The manager sends us all home by taxi now for as long as the murderer's on the loose.'

'A wise precaution,' Linus agreed absent-mindedly. 'Is there someone to show me to my room?'

It didn't take Linus long to unpack his overnight bag and he was soon standing outside again in the noon sunshine. The bulk of the aptly named Square Tower rose up on his left, its Portland stone gleaming in the sunlight. Linus turned and walked the short remaining length of High Street until he stood before the landward-facing wall, its blank façade relieved only by a bust of Charles I in a circular niche above an inscription and the royal coat of arms. To the right of the massive structure stretched the medieval ramparts which had for so many centuries defended the city from sea-borne attack.

Linus, who could see no way of getting into the Tower from this side, went through the watergate in the ramparts and found himself looking at a small pier which was quite emphatically not medieval and which had landing stages at different levels, presumably to allow boats to tie up at different stages of the tide. That, at least, was Linus's interpretation because he couldn't immediately think of any other explanation, even though it struck him as potentially disastrous to tie up at high tide and be away too long . . .

Little use was being made of it just now. An elderly couple had brought collapsible picnic chairs and were sunning themselves on one of the concrete platforms, their eyes closed in sun worship. Lower down, on the bottom, longest and most viable of the landing stages sat two fishermen, their backs to each other, silently and hopefully waiting. Linus hesitated. Anglers were reluctant conversationalists. Then he walked towards them and stood quietly watching for several minutes. There was no sign that either of them had caught anything.

'Biting?' he asked when he judged he had proved his basic lack of loquacity.

One of the two just grinned and nodded his head in the direction of his empty basket. The other kept his eyes on his line and said, 'Not so's you'd notice.'

Linus watched them in silence for several more minutes before again breaking the silence.

'Typical?'

The first man shrugged. The second said, 'Varies. Gets you away from the old woman, though.'

'Ah,' Linus said. 'Good point.'

After a few more minutes during which Linus made no attempt to go away, the second man turned his head and looked at him curiously. 'Was there something you wanted, mate?' he asked.

Linus remembered the receptionist's misconception. 'Journalist,' he said laconically. 'They wanted a piece on what the place is like afterwards—were people staying away or flocking around. That sort of thing.'

'You mean the murder the other night?'

Linus nodded.

'They closed it off for about twenty-four hours and they say folks was flocking to look. When they opened it up again, anything that was there had been taken away and the whole place hosed down. Nothing to see. It soon lost its interest.'

Linus nodded again. 'Where was it, exactly.'

'Not really sure. Where those two are sitting, I think.'

'Doesn't seem to be worrying them,' Linus commented.

'No reason why it should. Mind you, I don't think courting couples will be coming here much for the time being. Not until they catch him.'

When Linus returned that evening after dinner, the pier

was deserted and it seemed a much less friendly place in the dark of the chill night air. It wasn't just the air that made him shiver. Whatever had Miriam been doing here after dark? His visit was a brief one and his emergence through the watergate was met by a uniformed policeman who had been unobtrusively patrolling the casemates on the landward side of the ramparts.

'Fine evening, sir,' he said politely.

'A bit too chilly for me,' Linus told him.

'Local, are we, sir?'

The use by those in authority of the first person plural even when it couldn't conceivably apply to the speaker never failed to irritate Linus, but there was never any point in arguing semantically with the police, so he merely said, 'No, I arrived this morning. Putting up at the Dolphin.'

'Ah. Very nice, I've heard. Stayed there before?'

'Once. Three or four years ago. Yes, it's very comfortable.'

'Long stay, sir?'

'I doubt it. I've got be back at my desk on Monday.'

The policeman sighed in sympathy. 'Necessary evil, work. Just a little break, I take it?'

'Something like that. Bit of an impulse, I suppose. I like the seaside, you see. Mind you, I go off it when it's as chilly as this.'

'Then I'll not keep you in idle chit-chat, sir. You'll be wanting to get back to your hotel. Good night, sir.'

'Good night, Constable.'

Linus smiled to himself. Whatever the policeman had been indulging in, idle chit-chat played no part in it. Linus had no doubt at all that, until Miriam's killer was caught, anyone loitering round the Square Tower would be similarly and equally courteously grilled. Nor did he doubt that he would hardly have disappeared through the Dolphin's doors before the constable would be on his radio to his colleagues, a call that would very shortly be followed by a discreet check at the Dolphin on Linus's information. It wasn't a particularly subtle or sophisticated way of tracking down a murderer, since its only hope of success would be for that person first to return to the scene of the crime, and secondly to fail to see what the policeman was there for and to lie. Linus doubted whether many murderers were quite that stupid. On the other hand, it had to be done, if only to ensure some background information if history should repeat itself.

Back in his room, Linus lay on his bed, his arms behind his head, staring up at the ceiling. In an odd sort of way, he was glad he had come. He had learnt nothing new, but then he hadn't really expected to. He hadn't seen anything much, but then, if he was absolutely honest, he couldn't imagine what there would have been to see. It was as if, having made the pilgrimage, he had somehow expiated the greater part of his irrational feelings of guilt, had demonstrated to Miriam—or to her spirit, if one believed in that sort of thing—that he cared what happened to her even if their friendship had been brief and more superficial than perhaps he would initially have chosen.

There was nothing to keep him here any longer but now that he had made the effort, he'd stay another day. The break would do him good and he was only sorry that the present anti-dog climate had induced him to board Ishmael with the Thelwalls. Ishmael would have loved the break, too. Still, he'd stay tomorrow and be a tourist, then he'd go home first thing on Saturday morning.

It was a good day for being a tourist. The sun was warm enough to make a jacket superfluous yet not so warm as to be uncomfortable, and a slight sea breeze lifted the air, stirring the fragrances of the flowers in the ornamental gardens that separated the seafront hotels in their Victorian splendour from the esplanade. Linus knew of no other resort that had hit on this extremely civilized layout and decided that it, and the splendid view of the Isle of Wight, more than compensated for the shingle beach. If this were sand, he thought, the place would be perfect.

The Isle of Wight. Somewhere on that hump of land was Raymond March's other home, the place that had no neighbours and two Slovenian Mastiffs. Linus considered taking the hovercraft over and seeing whether he could track it down, just out of curiosity but he decided against it. Although it was probably on this, the north-facing side of the island, if only for ease of access, he had absolutely no idea whereabouts or even what it was called. Even if he hired a car for the day and scoured the lanes, he might well find several houses that fitted the few criteria he had but he was unlikely to be able to identify any of them as March's. He could ask around in local shops, of course, but since his interest was at best pure, unadulterated nosiness, he simply didn't have the gall. If he had believed there to be any truth in Miriam's story that March had a secret hoard of stolen Nazi art treasures, maybe he would, or if he thought March had any connection with her death. He smiled to himself. March had struck him as a fastidious man. He couldn't see him dirtying his hands with what had, by all accounts, been a singularly messy murder.

The discus thrower might. Linus called the man to mind. He was inclined to think he would have preferred a cleaner method—a straightforward shooting, perhaps—but at a push . . . yes, Linus was inclined to think the young Adonis had it in him, in which case it was reasonable to assume it would have been because they had found out that she knew March's secret and decided to silence her.

Linus smiled to himself. Once one started speculating melodramatically, there was no knowing the imaginative excesses to which it would lead. He visualized putting this hypothesis to the sharp-faced Netley and then visualized all too easily that man's politely disbelieving set-down.

He skimmed some pebbles across the water. It was a knack like riding a bicycle or swimming. Once acquired, it was never lost and there was something infinitely satisfying when it was done successfully. A ferry passed and Linus stopped to watch for the wash and its inevitable effect on the sailing dinghy it had overtaken.

As he narrowed his eyes against the sun to watch the bobbing of the small boat, his attention was drawn to the backdrop of the incident. A circular stone structure stood apparently midway between the beach and the Island and both boats had passed between this unlikely edifice and the shore. In the distance he could make out another, seemingly identical structure away to his left. It was difficult to judge their size, but they were much too big to be any sort of buoy or even a light-ship.

Linus ploughed his way laboriously back up the shingle and treated himself to an ice-cream from one of the kiosks.

'What's that thing out there, in the middle of the water?' he asked.

The girl's eyes followed his pointing finger. 'That? That's Spit Bank, I think. You can go on trips over it nowadays.'

'Are they worth going on?'

She shrugged. 'How should I know? They seem to get plenty of takers, though.'

'Is that another one over there?'

'There's four of them all told. I think the other two are closer to the Island.' She nodded in the direction of the one nearest to them. 'That's the only one you can go over, though.'

'What are they, exactly? Some kind of lighthouse?'

She looked puzzled. Perhaps she didn't want to tell a visitor not to be daft. 'I don't think so. I've never heard that. Don't know what they are now—except that one, of course: that's a tourist attraction. They were forts of some kind originally, I think.'

'I don't suppose you know how one goes about seeing over this one?'

She jerked her head towards the west. 'Clarence Pier. They sell tickets there. You'll see the notices.'

Linus walked along the promenade to the fun fair and bought himself a ticket. Then he joined the small queue waiting for the boat that took groups of about twenty at a time out to the fort. It was the perfect day for a trip in an open motorboat and Linus decided that even if the fort proved a dead loss, the trip there and back would have been worthwhile. The journey took longer than he had anticipated, but as they approached Spit Bank he could see that his original guess that it was midway between the Isle of Wight and the mainland was considerably out. It was much closer to the mainland.

Linus had a great fondness for architectural oddities. He had loved St Pancras Station even when it was unfashionable. He preferred follies to the great houses in whose gardens they stood unless the great house was itself a folly, like Waddesdon, the French château erected on a man-made hill in Buckinghamshire by one of the more original Rothschilds.

Spit Bank was bizarre enough to satisfy the most demanding of connoisseurs and Linus loved it. The basic plan was simplicity itself. There were two floors and a roof grouped round a central open well. The building was circular. The gun floor consisted of an outer circle of gun emplacements and an inner one of men's quarters, latrines, guardrooms and so on. Below that, the basement floor consisted of an outer circle of shell stores, each with its lift for transferring the ammunition to the relevant gun above, and half a dozen general storerooms. An inner circle of cartridge stores was separated from the outer one by a circular passage, half of it for shifting shells and the other for shifting stores. The roof of this passage was of variable height and while Linus didn't mind ducking his head, he wasn't too happy when he had to bend over to go any further. It wasn't that he suffered from claustrophobia, precisely—he was perfectly happy in the London Underground, for example—but he had always been conscious of a slight feeling of something very close to panic in an unnecessarily confined space. He often thought he would have no problems climbing mountains, if the urge to do so came upon him, but potholing . . . ugh! He couldn't even bear to watch other people doing it on television. No, he didn't like the shell passage.

He was intrigued at the forethought that had gone into much of the planning, especially the fact that the original oil lamps had been housed for safety's sake in glass-fronted niches, and that an artesian well had been sunk over four hundred feet into fresh water below the sea-bed. Thirst would not have killed men under siege.

Before they were taken back upstairs, the group was led into the general artillery store on this basement floor where they were shown what was referred to as the 'secret' of Spit Bank. There was a small opening in what should have been the outer wall of the fort, approached down a flight of steps. It led to something called a bolt passage, a narrow, two-feet wide, damp and windowless passage that led right round the circumference of the basement floor between what they had taken to be the outer wall and the outer wall proper. It had been built into the fort in case it became necessary to add iron armour to the lower part. This had never been done and it remained an oddity with just the one entrance point. The electricity that had been fitted elsewhere was quite absent from the bolt passage but candles in wine bottles stood on a table by the entrance and the tourists were invited to take one and follow the passage round.

'You can't get lost,' the guide assured them. 'It goes right round and comes out here.'

Like everyone else, Linus put his head into the passage and looked along it in each direction as far as the curve permitted, and then, like almost everyone else, he decided it was not for him and made his way back upstairs leaving an intrepid band of three to face the confining horrors of the passage.

The views from the roof were spectacular, though there was surprisingly little open space from which to enjoy it, due largely to the fact that the roof, which was extremely broad, sloped seawards at an angle on which it would probably be quite safe to walk, but less than advisable.

It was an interesting building and the present owners had put an enormous amount of effort, to say nothing of money, into restoring it as closely as they could to what it had been. Abandoned for forty years before the government found a buyer, gulls had come in through broken gun-ports and nested inside, leaving droppings over a metre deep to be removed as the first step in the fort's rehabilitation.

The tour over, they were free to wander round until the boat brought the next group across and Linus amused himself by deciding what he would do with it if it were his. There was no denying that, given enough money and enough imagination, to say nothing of a first-class architect, it could be turned into a very desirable residence. Well, Linus had the imagination and he had no doubt he could find the right architect. It was the money that would be the major stumbling block. Even a vet in private practice—a licence to print money these days, if ever there was one—wouldn't be able to rise to it. The fact that there was not the slightest danger he would ever be called upon to turn this dream into reality meant that he could indulge it to his heart's content. Which was, Linus thought, the best kind of dream to have.

*

Linus returned to work after the weekend completely restored. The break had been a good idea and not only because it had enabled him to accept the fact, if not the brutality, of Miriam's death. They had, after all, been very little to each other and when he looked at it rationally, he realized it had been as much the shock of the unexpected that had upset him as anything else. He would have felt the same had it been a colleague and it would probably have taken longer to come to terms with because every day there would be reminders of a colleague's former presence. There were no reminders of Miriam.

It was some two weeks after his visit to Portsmouth that he had a phone call. The voice was male, the accent American.

'Do I have the pleasure of speaking to Linus Rintoul?' it inquired with the excessive respectful formality some Americans adopt towards strangers.

'I've no idea,' Linus replied. 'But I'm Linus Rintoul, all right.'

The voice sounded puzzled. Linus guessed the brain behind it was trying to sort out his first sentence. 'The Linus Rintoul who works for—' there was a pause as if the speaker was referring to notes—'for the Ministry of Agriculture, Fisheries and Food?'

Definitely notes, Linus decided. Almost no one referred to it by its complete and cumbersome title. MAFF; Min of Ag; at most, Ministry of Agriculture. 'I do work there,' he admitted. 'And so far as I know I'm the only employee of that name.'

'You are a veterinary surgeon?' Again the full phrase and not the popular abbreviation. Again the doubt as to whether the speaker had the right man, as if Linus Rintouls grew in every back garden.

'I'm a vet,' Linus told him. 'So far as I know, I'm the only one in the book with that name.'

'I don't suppose you were by any chance acquainted with a lady called Miriam Greentree?'

Linus jumped. He might have expected to read the name in a newspaper; he wouldn't have been surprised if Netley returned with some more questions, especially once the report from the constable in Portsmouth filtered back to him. He did not expect to hear it from a total stranger over the phone.

'Who is this speaking?' he asked.

'I'm afraid my name won't mean anything to you,' the voice replied, apparently with sincere regret. 'Did you know her?'

Linus noted the use once again of the past tense. 'Yes, I knew a Miriam Greentree.'

'Good. I'm a colleague of hers. I wondered if we could meet sometime and have a chat.'

'Why would you want to do that?'

'There is a small problem I think you may be able to help us with.'

'Then you might as well fire away now,' Linus suggested.

'I don't think so. Not on the telephone, if it's all the same to you.'

'Where do you suggest?' Linus wasn't at all sure he had any intention of keeping any proposed rendezvous but his curiosity had been stirred.

The voice named a pub that Linus knew by sight but had never patronized. It lay on the edge of a village some miles to the east of the city; a village which had been stranded by the opening of the M40. It had become a purely dormitory village and was virtually dead during the day-time. He doubted if it was very much more lively at night. The voice suggested lunch the next day.

No, Linus thought. I don't know what this is about but I'm damned if I'm going to be too keen to meet him. He audibly ruffled the pages of the phone book and hoped it sounded like his desk diary. 'Sorry, I can't make tomorrow.'

'The next day?'

Linus sounded doubtful. 'Not for sure. Office conference. Can't be sure when it will finish. No, best not to make an appointment then.'

'I don't want to leave it too long. When do you suggest?'

Linus conceded that the day after would probably be all right. 'And your number if something comes up?' he asked.

'Don't worry. If you don't make it I'll ring again.'

'Fine. So who am I looking for?'

'No hassle. I know you by sight. One o'clock. I'll see you.' He hung up before Linus could press the matter.

Someone else who didn't give phone numbers—or addresses, either, most likely. Linus wondered why people did that. Did all this secrecy make them feel important or did they relish the sense of power it gave them to know that, while they could contact an individual whenever they wanted to, the individual concerned was not only unable to contact them, but was entirely dependent upon them for any continuance of the acquaintance? There was, of course, a third possibility. There might be some quite genuine security reason for not passing such particulars on. After all, if Linus didn't know who he was meeting or what the man's phone number was, he couldn't let it slip. Linus tried to imagine a situation in which he might be tempted to do so, but he failed.

Over the next two days he more than once regretted having played hard-to-get because his curiosity, having been aroused, began to work overtime. He didn't let it take over completely, however, and by not leaving the office until five to one, made sure that he arrived late enough for it to be The Voice who was getting anxious.

The only customer in the lounge bar did not strike Linus

as the victim of anxiety. The corn-fed jaw and the cut of his suit—an incongruous garment in a country pub at lunch-time—proclaimed his nationality and if his well-scrubbed face and his short, neat hair reminded Linus of anything, it was of a Mormon door-to-door proselytizer.

'Mr Rintoul,' he said, rising to his feet with the deference due to seniority. He held out his hand. 'David Huning. It's good of you to spare me the time. What will you have?'

Linus said half a pint of mild would do him very well and decided that the American wasn't as young as he had at first thought. Like Miriam, he was dark-haired and dark-eyed but his face was longer and Linus judged him to be about the same age. He noticed that the man had chosen a table as far removed from the bar as it was possible to be.

Linus thanked him for the beer when it arrived and took a good long draught. It was a warm day. 'That's better,' he said. 'Now, what's this all about?'

'You knew Miriam quite well, I believe?'

'We had dinner or lunch together a few times. I wouldn't claim to have known her quite well. In fact, I didn't know her well at all. It was a purely social acquaintance. Very pleasant, and all that, but there was no exchange of confidences.'

David Huning nodded. 'Miriam was a very private person,' he said.

Linus winced inwardly at the expression and hoped his pain didn't show on his face. He would have called her close.

'However,' Huning went on, 'I gather she told you something of our business.'

Linus's interest sharpened. The only thing about which she had been remotely forthcoming had been stolen works of art. 'What business would that be?' he asked cautiously.

'I think she said you shared an interest in art.'

Linus was tempted to ask him to define 'interest'. Interest in a subject implied a degree of background knowledge which in Linus's opinion, Miriam totally lacked. 'I sometimes buy pictures,' he said warily. 'Miriam had some sort of interest in a dealer with whom I was doing business.'

The American gave a smile that managed to combine confidentiality with a knowingness that was as significant as a finger-tap to the side of the nose would have been. He lowered his voice still further. 'I think you know a little more about it than that, Mr Rintoul.'

'I don't *know* anything,' Linus said tartly. 'She spun me some yarn. It wasn't one I necessarily believed.'

'It struck you as a shade improbable?'

'It struck me as several shades improbable.'

'But you didn't say as much to her?'

'What would have been the point? She was hardly likely to turn round and admit she'd made it up.'

'And what if I assured you it was the truth?'

Linus studied him thoughtfully. The man didn't look like a liar and he sounded as sincere as a television evangelist, in the way that only Americans can manage. Con-men, Linus reflected, would not be successful unless they could lie with convincing sincerity but he couldn't see what Huning had to gain by conning him. 'I'm not sure that I'd believe you, either.'

'And if I could convince you?'

'Then, in view of Miriam's rather unpleasant death, I'd suggest you tell the police.'

'At this stage it's just theory. They'd probably be as dismissive as you.'

'Just theory? That wasn't the impression Miriam gave me. She didn't seem to be in much doubt about it.'

'Not much doubt, no. Proof is something else.'

'The police are admirably situated to find proof,' Linus pointed out.

'But they would require a firmer base to work from that we can offer them.'

'We?'

'I'm only part of the investigating team.'

'Was Miriam another part?'

'She was.' Huning looked at Linus's glass. 'Another one? Something to eat? They do a good ploughman's here, I believe.'

Linus was by no means convinced that the man wasn't some kind of nut-case, except for the fact that he was obviously connected with Miriam and must have been talking to her. He couldn't help wondering whether that talk had taken place on a deserted landing stage in Old Portsmouth. He wasn't particularly anxious to prolong this interview but, since he was here and since he was undoubtedly very hungry, he saw no reason why the cause of his trekking all this way shouldn't at least buy him lunch. 'A ploughman's wouldn't come amiss,' he said.

The door opened while Huning was at the bar and Linus recognized the man who came in. Inspector Lacock was a policeman with whom Linus got on reasonably well on those occasions when their professional paths crossed. Since he was in civvies, Linus deduced he was off duty, in so far as any policeman ever is.

Lacock paused by his table. 'You certainly get about the area, Rintoul,' he said.

'You're some way adrift yourself, aren't you?' Linus replied.

'Don't I know it! House-hunting. At least, I'm making the preliminary sortie. The wife has a fancy to live out this way. Says it'll be easier to reach London.'

'Not a place too many men would want to encourage their wives to visit,' Linus remarked, thinking of the shops.

'Quite, but it's more than my life's worth to say so. She's being magnanimous. Hands me a fistful of agents' guff and says "You sort out the ones you'd be happiest with and then we'll go over them together." Trouble is, if I take her at her word, I'm bound not to select the very one she thought was the most promising.'

'So what do you do?'

'I have a quick shufti round three or four and then tell her it's an impossible choice and I need her impression. Then she throws away the details of those she doesn't like the sound of anyway, and I lose my precious free time going over the rest.'

'Why not let her do the initial sorting out? It's what most wives do.'

'Because she knows I don't want to move at all. If she does that, she'll be continually claiming she feels guilty because perhaps I'd have preferred one of the others. I tried saying I don't want any of them, but I gather that's just being obstructive. I don't think I can win. Are you on your own?'

'No.' Huning was on his way back to the table with their lunches. 'Huning—Lacock,' Linus said and both men nodded at each other. Linus very nearly added, 'Lacock's a policeman. Why don't you test your theory on him?' He didn't, because he knew that policemen off duty are not happy to have all and sundry told what they do for a living. Tax-men had the same hang-up.

'I'll leave you to get on with your meal,' Lacock said and when he had been served at the bar, took his pint to the corner opposite the other two.

'Friend of yours?' Huning said.

'Acquaintance.' Linus wondered if it was just his imagination that Huning sounded suspicious.

'Odd coincidence. Him being here, I mean.'

'They do happen,' Linus said, unperturbed.

All the same, the presence of someone who knew Linus seemed to deter Huning from returning to the subject of their previous conversation, and he kept to general topics. Had Linus ever visited the States? No? He really should. New England in the fall was particularly worth a visit. Pennsylvania had much to offer and of course, as a vet, the Blue Grass country of Kentucky would just enchant him.

Linus, who doubted it very much, made diplomatically noncommittal replies and discovered that Huning was at least as adept at keeping this sort of conversation going as Miriam had been. He supposed it was a social asset and wondered whether he ought to acquire it.

Not until Lacock had finished his pint and left the pub, nodding goodbye as he went out, did Huning return to the subject previously in hand.

'The thing is, Mr Rintoul, I have a hunch you and me can do business.'

'I doubt it,' Linus told him. 'Business really isn't my forte.'

Huning looked briefly puzzled and then gave the polite smile that indicates recognition that a joke has been made and at the same time a total absence of any comprehension what the joke was about. 'I guess that must be your English sense of humour,' he said.

'Quite probably,' Linus agreed. 'What exactly are you on about?'

Huning frowned. 'On about?' he echoed. 'I'm not familiar with English idioms.'

'No. I'd noticed,' Linus said sardonically. 'I meant what do you mean? What is the nature of this business you think we can do together or between us, or each on our own?'

The pedantry which Linus lapsed into when he was irritated was lost on his audience whom it merely mystified, but he got the gist.

'As I said, we're fairly sure . . . your dealer friend . . . is at the heart of this art caper but we need proof. We think you're the perfect person to find that proof.'

'Let's get this straight,' Linus said firmly. 'Is this the royal "we" or do you have colleagues?'

'I have colleagues.'

'And who may they be?'

'Ah, that, I'm afraid, is something I'm not at liberty to reveal.'

'Suitably mysterious. All right, I'll not press that for the moment. What makes you think I'm the person for the job?'

'You know pictures and you're familiar with the art world.'

'On a peripheral and entirely amateur basis,' Linus pointed out. 'I'm hardly the person to authenticate anything.'

'We can find experts for that,' the American assured him. 'More importantly, those qualifications have already introduced you to Raymond March. He knows you collect. You've bought from him once. He will be quite ready to believe you're looking for something else.'

Linus shook his head. 'You're deluding yourself. He's a very shrewd man. He knows perfectly well I can afford pictures in his price range only once in a blue moon.'

'But he's not going to discourage your interest, just in case, is he? You see, we're reasonably sure he doesn't keep the stolen pictures at the Henley gallery or at the Henley house. I think you know he has another house?'

'I had heard. Very isolated, I believe.'

'Very. It's also well-guarded and virtually impossible to approach unseen. We need to know *exactly* where those works of art are so that we can go straight to them.'

'Do you fondly imagine he's going to take a small-time collector he scarcely knows by the hand and say, "Come and look in my secret vaults. I've got a nice little Rubens or Titian or Vermeer I think you'll fall for. I'm sure your bank manager will oblige"? Don't be stupid.' Linus was tempted to add, 'And don't take me for a fool, either,' but he didn't. After all, the man had just bought him lunch.

David Huning shifted uneasily. 'I agree that it sounds ridiculous, put like that. The thing is, being sure the pictures are there, and their precise whereabouts within the building, are only part of it. We don't have any doubt at all that March is involved at the disposal end. What we want is evidence to link him with the other end.'

'You mean evidence that will prove he was involved in the original theft or concealment—or both?'

'Exactly.'

'Presumably one would first have to find proof that he was a German by birth, a Nazi, and in the Wehrmacht or the SS, or something?'

'That's right.'

'Hmm. You'd better team up with the Kennel Club.'

Linus hadn't intended the remark to leave the man quite so gob-smacked but there was no denying it was extremely gratifying to have shaken that earnest smugness. Until this moment, Linus had been very conscious that Huning had the upper hand because he also had the information. He had also realized that all the objections he put forward had been anticipated and the counter-arguments rehearsed. It was good to see that balance shaken.

'The Kennel Club?' Huning echoed. 'What have they got to do with it?'

'He's a member. Didn't you know?'

'Yes, of course, but I don't see . . .'

'They've got their own reasons for being interested in his age. Why don't you get in touch with them? After all, if he's only sixty-five, as he claims, he was only twelve in 1939 and barely eighteen at the end of the war. Unlikely, I would have thought, to have got himself into a position of sufficient trust to be involved at the level you suggest. Oh, as an unimportant private he might well have been one of those who lugged crates from A to B, but he wouldn't have known what was in them. Of course, if he's really seventy—or better still, seventy-five—the degree of involvement is likely to be closer to what you have in mind. Maybe you should approach them. Maybe their inquiries are further ahead than yours. Maybe you can work together for your mutual benefit.'

Huning was silent, trying to slot this new piece into a game of which he thought he had the mastery.

'I don't think so,' he said at last. 'I think we'd best stick to our original scenario. If you want to make a bit on the side letting this Kennel Club know his age when you've found it out, that's fine by us.' He paused and his face suddenly cleared as if a problem had been solved. 'You will be paid for your time, of course. Generously paid.'

'You seem to be forgetting that I've already got a day job.'

The American shrugged. 'Take a vacation. Call in sick. Who's to know?'

'I'd know.'

'We're talking cash in hand here. No records, to tax liability.'

Linus pushed his plate away and stood up. 'It gets more and more suspect every time you open your mouth. No, thank you, Mr Huning. I'm totally unqualified for what you want me to do; I've got a job I like and for which I *am* qualified and a salary with which I'm entirely happy.' Well, he thought, at least the first two statements are truthful. 'I also have a constitutional dislike of having my skull smashed in with a blunt instrument. Find yourself another Miriam Greentree.'

Huning seized on a weakness of which no man, in his experience, would be willing to stand accused. 'Are you telling me you're chicken, Mr Rintoul? A red-blooded man like you?'

'That's right,' Linus said cheerfully. 'And the blood's

yellow. Runs in the family. Hereditary abnormality.' He chuckled at a professional joke. 'Goodbye, Mr Huning, and thank you for lunch. I'm sorry you've been wasting your time.'

Linus drove back to the office too fast for safety. This was the result of annoyance rather than of two halves of mild. He was annoyed that his time had been wasted and annoyed at the assumption that his time could be bought if the offer could be made sufficiently tempting. Very American, he thought. He was also uneasy, though not for his life. Miriam had been up to something. He hadn't known what and he certainly hadn't believed her story about Nazi loot. Now here was someone else with exactly the same story. Linus still thought it was preposterous but the seeds of doubt had been sown. What if it were true? After all, it wasn't entirely outside the bounds of possibility. No one had ever disputed that the Nazis had looted the palaces and museums of the countries they had overrun and that most of this stolen property had vanished without trace. Some items purporting to be lost works had resurfaced after the war and been snapped up by the institutions from which they had been taken without too many questions being asked, including, in some cases, about their authenticity—or so it was said. It was reasonable to assume that those missing pictures must be somewhere and they couldn't all be in the hands of that largely mythical individual, the mad private collector who gloated over his acquisitions in the deepest privacy. Quite apart from anything else, such collectors were as mortal as the next man and their pictures were likely to come to light when they died.

It was unlikely that the lost masterpieces were all to be found in one place, although it was reasonable to assume that there might be several large caches hidden around

Europe. Continental Europe, that is. Given the circumstances, England must be just about the least likely place to find them. Not even the Isle of Wight. Now if Raymond March's other home had been on Alderney . . .

It was all very well to speculate on the possibility of the story being true. Such speculation did nothing to explain Miriam Greentree and David Huning. Miriam's attempts to track down the pictures seemed to be limited to following March around, even to the quarantine kennels, and Linus couldn't see that that could have got her very much further. Now Huning had approached him, a virtual stranger. Who or what, exactly, were Miriam and Huning? Interpol? Linus thought about that and decided it was improbable. He had no idea whether Interpol had the slightest on-going interest in works stolen nearly half a century ago but he was reasonably sure that if they had, they could produce detectives who were complete experts in their field, and that was something Miriam Greentree had emphatically not been. He was also absolutely certain that the last thing Interpol would be likely to do would be to approach a layman—'lay' both with reference to art and to police work—who was a total stranger and try to enlist his help. No, they weren't Interpol.

It was far more likely that Miriam and Huning had been freelances. Treasure-hunters, perhaps, whose 'colleagues' were quite simply those who put up the money. All they would be interested in would be in finding where the pictures were kept and then, presumably after meticulous planning, steal them themselves in order to filter them back on to the legitimate market in precisely the way March was supposed to be doing, and thereby making a handsome profit for them and their 'colleagues'. A variation on this scenario, to use Huning's word, would be to assume that the investing 'colleagues' wanted the pictures for their own private collections, which, Linus thought, brings us neatly back to the mad collector syndrome.

Wherever the truth lay, one thing emerged in Linus's estimation as incontrovertible. Miriam and Huning were not on the level and he was well out of it. He fingered his beard and the patchwork of healed scars it hid. Chicken he might well be, but at least he wasn't stupid.

CHAPTER 7

Linus put the whole peculiar business out of his mind over the next few days. It was bizarre and if it was true it was almost certainly crooked. That was enough for him.

Vets in private practice may curse when the phone rings at one o'clock in the morning but they aren't surprised. Such calls are no more likely to occur in the life of a government vet than in that of any other member of the community and Linus had long ago got out of the habit of waking the instant it rang if it did so at night. First it had to penetrate his deep sleep and when it had done so, he lay there in a befuddled haze wondering if he was really hearing it or whether it was part of a dream that had strayed over into his consciousness. When he decided it was real, he pondered the possibility that it was next door's phone, a theory that had to be rejected because it was too clear, too intrusive; and then wondered whether he had left the television on. By this time his thoughts were clear enough for him to conclude that it couldn't be the television because telephones in films never rang as persistently as this.

It was his phone. It was still ringing. Somebody must be trying to contact him urgently. Therefore it must be important. Someone was hurt. One of the children.

Linus threw back the bedclothes, leapt out of bed and

raced down the stairs to reach the phone before the caller finally gave up.

'Mr Rintoul?'

The voice was vaguely familiar but he couldn't place it. 'Speaking.'

'You took your time.'

The voice had American undertones. Huning? At this hour? 'What do you want? It's the middle of the night, for God's sake.'

'We're very disappointed in you, Rintoul. We thought you were a sensible man, a responsible citizen.'

Definitely Huning, Linus decided. Was the man trying to inveigle him into cooperating with him or was his intention to make Linus sorry he had declined his offer? Linus couldn't think of any other possibility and either way, the phone call was going to be counter-productive because all it did—now any anxiety about the children had been allayed—was to make him hopping mad at being woken up.

'Look here, Huning, I made myself perfectly clear. I'm not interested in playing your sort of games and if you're not prepared to leave it at that, I'll tell the whole story to the police.'

'I wouldn't do that, Mr Rintoul.' There was menace in the voice but also, Linus thought, a hint of fear.

'I'm sure you'd rather I didn't. I suspect you'd be lucky if the worst thing that happened to you was deportation. I'm beginning to think I should have gone to them straight away. Maybe I'll remember that. I'm certainly not putting up with having my sleep interrupted.'

'You would be very well advised to drop the whole matter, Mr Rintoul.'

'Which is precisely what I had done—until now.'

'We needed to check.' It was a statement rather than an explanation.

'At one o'clock in the morning? Balls!'

'It was the only way we could be sure of catching you at home. We would be very unhappy if you went to the police.'

'I'm sure you would. I'll think about it. It's not an option I'm prepared to rule out. Good night.' Linus slammed down the phone.

He went back to bed but found it difficult to sleep. It wasn't simply that the timing of the call had annoyed him. The call itself had unnerved him and he had little doubt that the timing of it had been calculated to do precisely that. He tossed and turned and considered whether to implement his threat of going to the police. It was a temptation but he couldn't face the endless repetitive questions and the overall disbelief. No, Huning had probably still been of the opinion that Linus could be persuaded to help and was very likely prepared to up the ante had he showed any inclination to change his mind. As to the implied threat, Linus dismissed it. It didn't much matter whether Huning's story was true or not: in neither case would he—or his invisible associates, if they existed—want the police brought in. Linus very much doubted that they would draw attention to themselves by doing away with him. There might be one or two more dead-of-night phone calls, but he could pre-empt that by unplugging the phone when he went to bed. As for getting back to sleep tonight, well, a stiff whisky would see to that.

Linus could hardly miss the report in the *Oxford Mail* of a body found floating face down in the Thames near Maidenhead because it occupied most of the front page. He read it because it was there to be read but it was not an unusual occurrence in itself, and the paper made no mention of any peculiarities likely to make it stick in the reader's mind. Linus promptly forgot about it and it was sheer chance that, several days later, his eye was drawn to a small paragraph on an inside page to the effect that the body had been identified as that of an American visitor, David Huning, and the police would welcome calls from anyone who had been in the region of the river around the time that he was believed to have fallen in.

Linus toyed briefly with the idea of telling them what he knew about the man but decided against it. He hadn't been at the river and he could throw no light at all on what had apparently been an accident or suicide. There was no mention of suspected foul play and, while it was an odd and uncomfortable coincidence that both Miriam and Huning should be dead, the manner of their deaths was so dissimilar that Linus was inclined to believe that they must be coincidental even though, on an intellectual level, he didn't have much faith in coincidences.

He wasn't one to wish sudden death on anyone, including David Huning, but at least it meant that he needn't worry about any more unnerving phone calls. Linus left the phone plugged in that night and had the first really sound night's sleep since Huning's call.

The front door always had been inclined to stick, though usually only in wet weather. This evening, though, it felt more as if something were wedged behind it.

Linus bent down and peered through the letter-box. He could see nothing. Except, craning his head to the right, he thought he could see the tip of Ishmael's brindle tail. It was a funny place for the dog to decide to sleep.

'Ishmael! Get up, Ishmael!' he called through the letter-box but there was no response.

Linus pushed a bit harder and this time the door moved. Not far, but enough to enable him to squeeze through.

He soon saw why Ishmael hadn't responded.

Ishmael was dead. Very dead indeed.

And natural causes had nothing to do with it. His head had been blown away. Linus knew enough forensic science to hazard an educated guess that someone had fired a gun straight into his open mouth, presumably having first knocked at the door, something that would naturally have brought the dog barking to see who it was. Now that he was looking for more than the cause of an obstruction, Linus noticed that the walls were spattered with bits of blood and brains and, presumably, fragments of bone as well. The same must be true of the carpet but it was dark brown and any blood had soaked into it.

Linus felt his stomach heave and he rushed into the kitchen to throw up in the sink. As a vet, he could face blood and guts with clinical objectivity but Ishmael was his pet, his much-loved companion. Clinical objectivity didn't enter into it. He found a sheet in the airing-cupboard and covered the dog with it while the professional in him took over. The easiest thing to do with it would be either to get the council to take the body away, which they wouldn't be able to do until next day, or he could take Ishmael out to Thelwall and ask him to incinerate him. Alternatively, he could bury him in the tiny garden.

This was the sentimental choice but Linus felt sentimental about the dog even though this particular garden was a far from ideal place. There was a shovel in the car. He stepped over the sheet and fetched it.

It takes time to dig a hole deep enough to bury even a small dog and Ishmael wasn't small. As he dug, Linus had plenty of time to try and work out not so much what had happened—about which there was little doubt—but why, and it was no bad thing that the sheer effort involved in digging Ishmael's grave went a long way towards working off the fury Linus felt.

He could think of only one feasible explanation. Ishmael was a Pit Bull Terrier. Worse, he had originally been a fighting dog. His origins were no secret among either Linus's friends or his neighbours and, since he took very good care never, ever, to let the dog off the lead if there was even the remotest chance of their meeting another dog or even people, Ishmael had given him not one moment's anxiety since he had given him a home to save him being put down.

The ownership of Pit Bulls was now virtually illegal. Linus had already castrated Ishmael in anticipation of the legislation that would govern those kept as pets and was trying to accustom the dog to a muzzle, distressing though that was for both of them. All the same, there was no denying that the country was becoming increasingly and neurotically virulent against dogs and particularly against any that were perceived as posing a possible threat. It seemed more than likely that one of these moronic neuropaths had decided to rid the world of at least one of the objects of his—the method of destruction argued against its being a woman—obsession.

It was dark before Ishmael was buried and Linus was free to turn his attention to the even more unpleasant task of cleaning up the house, but he knew he couldn't go to bed without having done it. He wondered whether any useful purpose would be served by calling on his neighbours to find out whether they had seen or heard anything but decided against it. No one would have been likely to walk the streets of Osney Mead carrying anything larger than a well concealed hand-gun and since the killing must have been premeditated, it was reasonable to assume the weapon had been silenced. Linus had no idea how much difference this made in practice to the amount of noise, but guessed it would be easily drowned by the thickness of the walls and the noise of an adjacent television or radio. He guessed, too, that the killer would have made sure there was no one about when he crouched down to fire through the letter-box. Linus mentally reviewed his immediate neighbours who might have heard something—they would have heard

Ishmael bark, for instance—but would have been unlikely to see anything. It was a pity there were no houses opposite, only the river.

Linus cleaned and scrubbed and then cleaned again and when he had finished the house, he scrubbed himself as if by doing so he could expiate some guilt he felt but couldn't explain. Only when all that had been done could he face going to bed. He was totally exhausted by the evening's toil but sleep eluded him. The manner of Ishmael's death and the inevitable reflection upon the sickness of the society in which we now live combined to make him feel physically ill and night was well on its way towards morning before he was finally able to close his eyes.

Two days later among his post was an envelope which can have done nothing to improve the postman's eyesight, since the name and address had been printed by a very faint dot-matrix printer. Linus guessed it to be a circular. He knew people who slung them in the bin unopened. He lacked that sort of confidence in the unimportance of the contents and always opened them. It was not a circular and it was perfectly easy to read, the text being constructed in best TV-thriller style out of letters and words cut from newspapers and stuck on to a sheet of paper. The message was succinct.

REMEMBER THE DOG. KEEP YOUR NOSE OUT.

Linus's heart—or perhaps it was his stomach—lurched into his throat. So much for the moronic neuropath. Ishmael's death had nothing to do with his having been a Pit Bull Terrier. It would have been the same if he'd been a Chihuahua. It was another of Huning's little ploys.

Then he remembered that David Huning was dead and had been so long before Ishmael was killed or the letter posted.

He searched among the rest of that day's post for the

discarded envelope. There was no postmark. There wasn't even the row of blue dots that these days sometimes cancelled stamps. The first class stamp was unmarked. The letter could even have been popped through the letter-box by hand, stamped to mislead him into thinking it had been posted. More probably, it had quite simply slipped through the sorting office net. It told Linus nothing.

What should he do about it? Perhaps this was the time to bring in the police. Perhaps he should have contacted them when he'd found the dog. After all, nothing justifies such a killing in law. He had known it at the time, really, and hadn't because he knew it would be futile: they'd never find the nutter who did it, and the distress of going over it all for them was something he couldn't face. This put a different complexion on it altogether. The only drawback to telling the police now was that they would almost certainly want to dig Ishmael up. That wasn't going to hurt Ishmael, of course, and Linus didn't delude himself that animals had souls. No, it was Linus the disinterment would upset. He had to decide which upset him more. That, or the direct threat contained in the letter.

Another restless night left him still undecided but then the decision was taken away from him. He was washing up his breakfast things when a knock on the door brought him face to face once more with Detective-Inspector Netley and his bucolic sergeant.

'Good morning, Mr Rintoul. Glad to have caught you. May we come in?'

Linus wasted no breath on a reply. He simply stood aside and let them in. 'Tea?' he asked.

'A cup of coffee would go down very well if you have one,' Netley replied with uncharacteristic affability.

'So long as you don't mind instant.' Linus glanced at the sergeant. 'And you, Sergeant?'

'If it isn't too much trouble, sir, I'd prefer tea at this time in the morning.'

'No trouble.' Linus smiled to himself. His guess that the countryman would prefer tea had been correct and Netley's failure even to consult his partner was illuminating.

'Do you take the local paper, Mr Rintoul?' Netley asked when Linus returned with the tray.

'Yes. Both of them.'

'Good. Then you'll have seen that they found a body near Maidenhead.'

'I read something about it.'

'Perhaps you missed the paragraph a few nights later asking for anyone who knew him to come forward.'

Linus frowned. 'I must have done. I recall something about people who'd been near the river at that time being asked to contact you.'

'That's the bit. You didn't.'

'Because Osney Mead was as near the Thames as I would have been at the time. I was certainly nowhere near Maidenhead.'

'So you don't deny you knew David Huning?' Linus thought he detected a note of subdued triumph in the detective's voice.

'If that's who he was, then I was acquainted with someone of that name. It would be a bit of an overstatement to say I knew him.'

'Just how well did you know him?'

'I met him once. We had lunch in a pub. Inspector Lacock dropped in and I think I introduced them to each other.'

'Had you arranged to meet Huning there or was it a chance meeting?'

'It was an arrangement. He'd rung me up.'

'Out of the blue?'

'Completely.'

'He must have given some sort of reason for wanting to meet you.'

'We had a friend in common.' If Netley had been Lacock, Linus knew he would quite simply have sat down and told him the whole improbable story, but Netley wasn't Lacock. Linus didn't trust him, although he had no grounds for not doing so and even though he was prepared to acknowledge that his mistrust was more a matter of incompatible personalities than anything else. Such considerations made no difference. So far as Linus was concerned, Netley could work for every sliver of information.

'Perhaps you'd give me the name of this mutual friend,' Netley suggested.

'Common friend,' Linus corrected pedantically. 'Certainly. It was Miriam Greentree.'

'Ah, yes, the young lady who also met a rather unexpected end. So she put you in touch with Huning?'

'No, the other way round. She never mentioned him to me.'

'But you had no reason to doubt an association between them when he contacted you?'

Linus hadn't but it was difficult after this interval to recall precisely why. 'I know he mentioned her by name. I think he said she was a colleague,' he said at last.

'So why did he want to meet you? To reminisce about Ms Greentree?'

Linus frowned, trying to recall. 'No. He said something about having a problem to discuss.'

'It didn't occur to you that this might have had something to do with her death and that you should have reported his call to us?'

'No,' Linus said after thinking about it. 'It didn't cross my mind.'

Netley seemed to accept the explanation. 'And what was this problem?'

Linus sighed. 'With your permission, Detective-Inspector, I'll ring the office and tell them I'm going to be in late, at best. Then I shall try to explain this rather bizarre and highly improbable story from the beginning.'

Netley's smile was almost warm. 'I wish you would, Mr Rintoul. You've no idea how exhausting it is having to drag every tiny snippet out of you, a piece at a time. If I may make a small suggestion: while you're up, some more tea and coffee all round wouldn't come amiss. It sounds as if this might be a long haul.'

When Linus returned to the sitting-room with the tray, he detailed as succinctly as he could, the sequence of events from his first visit to March's gallery to his rejection of Huning's offer. He didn't mention the very minor side issue of the Kennel Club's concern over the man's age because it was, in his estimation, just that: a side issue and not germane to the wider story. He kept to the facts. It was long enough in the telling without going into his own reactions.

When he had finished, Netley studied him in silence for a while. 'You're an intelligent man, Mr Rintoul,' he said at last and, when Linus modestly demurred, added, 'You must be: you're a qualified vet. Are you telling us you swallowed this Greentree woman's story?'

'No, I'm not. I'm just telling you what the story was. I didn't believe it at all.'

'Because it was too far-fetched?'

'There was that, of course, but no, that wasn't the reason. I mean, everyone knows works of art *were* stolen by the Nazis and most of them haven't been seen since the end of the war. They must be somewhere and it's a reasonable guess that they were hidden in caches and the person who finds one of those caches will do very well out of it. It was far-fetched but it wasn't impossible. No, the reason I didn't believe it was because, for someone supposedly on the track of lost works of art, she was not only surprisingly uninterested in paintings, but also remarkably ignorant.'

'For example?'

Linus told him about his cow. 'That's what made me discount her story. There was something else on that wall when I brought it back and I wasn't really sure where I wanted to hang the new one. I asked her what she suggested. It was as much a matter of courtesy as because I thought she'd come up with the ideal spot, you understand. Well, she glanced around and suggested over there. Right opposite the window.'

'What's wrong with that?' Netley asked. 'You'd be able to see it very clearly.'

'It's a watercolour. The last place you hang watercolours is facing direct light. They fade. It's an absolutely fundamental rule that anyone with any knowledge of pictures would know. They just wouldn't even consider such a position.'

Netley nodded and Linus guessed that the information was being mentally filed for future reference. 'Did that matter if all they wanted to do was to track March back to his alleged roots?'

'Perhaps not, but if the missing masterpieces were the reason for that search and if they were on the right trail, it's reasonable to assume that sooner or later she might come across some. Wouldn't it be essential to have on their trail someone with rather more than a passing knowledge of the field? Quite frankly, I doubt if she would have known an original drawing—or even watercolour—from a print or a pen-and-ink from an etching.'

'Then why do you think she spun you this yarn?'

'I haven't a clue. I wondered whether she was one of those people who make up fantastic stories to make themselves feel important but there's no doubt she *was* following March. Come to think of it, if I'd heard that the gallery had been burgled, I suppose her name would have sprung to mind, but that hasn't happened. Anyway, when she died, I decided that was the end of it and Huning came as a bolt from the blue.'

'Did you still disbelieve it?'

'Let's say my disbelief wavered. I decided that if March really did have one of those caches in his possession, Huning's interest was most likely in order to divert it into his possession instead. I wasn't sure that I believed him at all, but I was sure that whatever he was up to, it came under the heading of No Good and I wanted nothing to do with it.'

'Very laudable,' Netley murmured. 'So that was the one and only time you saw Huning?' Linus nodded. 'And you had no further contact from him?'

Linus hesitated. 'Not quite. I had a phone call; rather a threatening phone call, I suppose.' As accurately as he could recall, Linus gave Netley the details.

'You're quite sure this was Huning?' the policeman said when he had finished.

'Of course,' Linus replied, surprised. 'Who else could it have been?'

'Ah, does that mean it was an assumption on your part? Or did he introduce himself?'

'I assumed it to be him. It was the accent, you see.'

'Was that the only reason you assumed it was Huning? There are rather a lot of Americans in Britain and quite a number of them are in this area. Or did they actually recognize his voice?'

Linus considered that for several minutes. 'It was primarily the accent, I think. That and the fact that what he said fitted in quite well as a follow-up to our conversation. Perhaps that was the clincher. People don't necessarily sound quite the same on the phone. Sometimes you don't recognize their telephone voice until you've heard it several times.'

'Cast your mind back, Mr Rintoul. You say you assumed it was Huning though he didn't give his name. I don't suppose you gave him any indication of who you thought he was,'

That was a tricky question to answer, demanding a far more accurate recall facility than Linus possessed. 'I may have used his name,' he said doubtfully. 'I can't be sure. I'm quite sure I didn't say anything definite like "Is that you, Huning?" but I may have said something like, "Hello, Huning" or "Look here, Huning".' As he said the words, his recollection sharpened. 'Yes. Yes, I think that's exactly what I did say: "Look here, Huning."'

Netley wrote this down before responding. 'And since you're still convinced it was Huning you were speaking to, I assume he said nothing after that comment to disabuse you of the idea?'

'Obviously not.' Linus laughed ruefully. 'Which must be the real reason I never doubted his identity. Why? Do you think it was someone else?'

'Did the phone call worry you?' Netley said, ignoring the question.

'A little, I suppose. It was all quite clearly part of the melodramatic whole but that sort of threat leaves a nasty taste in the mouth.'

'But not nasty enough to come to us.'

'I thought about it. To be quite blunt, I didn't because I couldn't face going into all this improbable farrago to some politely incredulous policeman.'

'We do take threats seriously, Mr Rintoul.'

'I'm sure you do. You must also meet your full share of attention-seeking nutters. If I'd been getting threats as a MAFF vet, I wouldn't have thought twice about it because

I know it would have been taken seriously. But coupled with a yarn about hidden Nazi loot . . . ?'

The sergeant was grinning appreciatively. Linus guessed he was mentally putting himself in the position of the man who would have received the complaint. Even Netley managed a dry smile. 'I take your point, Mr Rintoul.'

'When the paper published the name of the drowned man, I have to say I heaved a sigh of relief,' Linus went on. 'I thought, right, that's it. Nothing to worry about on that score.' He shifted unhappily in his chair. 'This time I really was about to get in touch with you, only it can't have been Huning because he's dead.' As briefly as he could and with a desperate effort to keep his emotion under control, Linus told him about Ishmael, his assumption at the time and the letter he had received which put a rather different complexion on the whole business.

'You realize, of course, that we're going to have to exhume the dog,' Netley said.

'I know. That's the only reason I was hesitating.'

'You say the dog was shot. Obviously forensic will confirm this or not, as the case may be, but it can't be the first time you've seen an animal that had been killed that way. I don't suppose you could hazard a guess as to whether it was shot or a bullet?'

Linus shook his head. 'I didn't think it was a shotgun. I suppose in part because I assumed, given the fact that there are houses on either side and passers-by, that whatever weapon it was must have been silenced.'

'But you didn't look for a bullet?'

'The dog was dead, obviously shot. No, I didn't do a PM.'

'And when you cleaned up, you didn't come across a bullet? At that range it might well have gone straight through the dog.'

Linus shook his head. 'I didn't look, but I'd have noticed

a hole in the plaster, anything like that. No, nothing.'

'Bullets do funny things. We'll get them round. I'd be obliged if you'd not do any rooting around yourself. If there's anything here, we'd like to find it for ourselves. May the sergeant use your phone?'

Netley and his sergeant took Linus away while Ishmael was being exhumed. They needed a statement from him and he had to agree that it would be less distressing to be busy elsewhere than to watch.

'You'll be able to have him back when they've finished, sir,' the sergeant told him.

Linus shook his head. Somehow it was no longer important. 'No,' he said. 'Dispose of him in the usual way when you've finished.'

'Are you sure, sir? If you are, I'll tell them to fill in the hole again. That'll make it less distressing for you.'

'Thank you, Sergeant,' Linus said, genuinely grateful for the man's unexpected kindness. 'I'd appreciate that.'

In the interview room at St Aldate's police station, Linus made his statement. He was quite surprised that Netley remained in the room throughout. Linus would have thought it could have been left to minions thereby releasing the Detective-Inspector for something more important, especially since a third man in plain clothes and to whom Linus was not formally introduced was present throughout. Witness enough, one would have thought. Still, the deployment of police manpower was hardly Linus's province, except as one who contributed to their wages, and he wasn't in the right frame of mind to pursue that line of thought.

The statement took a long time to write and then to read through and when he had finished, Linus picked up his pen to sign it. He was surprised to have the statement whisked away.

'One moment, Mr Rintoul,' Netley told him. 'I have to ask if you're entirely satisfied this is an accurate statement.'

'Of course it is. It's only what I've already told you.'

'And it's complete? There's nothing else, upon mature reflection, that you'd like to add?'

Linus shook his head, puzzled. 'No.' Something in Netley's tone implied that Netley was aware of an omission and made Linus doubt, despite his certainty. He thought back over what he had told them. 'No, there's nothing else,' he said.

'You don't sound too sure.'

'Only because your tone made me think again.'

'And your second thoughts haven't produced anything new?'

'No.'

'You didn't see Huning again after the lunch when Inspector Lacock saw you together?'

'I've already told you, that was the one and only time I ever met him.'

'You didn't, so to speak, bump into him again?'

'No.'

'Mr Rintoul, we have here a man who came to you with what you yourself have described as a cock-and-bull story that wasn't entirely ubelievable and you decided that if it *was* true, then whatever he was up to was probably illegal and you wanted nothing to do with it. Right?'

'Right.'

'Then, when you think you've said no unequivocally enough to be satisfied he knows you mean it, you get a phone call telling you, in effect, to keep your mouth shut and, in particular, not to go to the police. By your own admission, this worried you.'

Linus nodded.

'Now you're a man who picks your words with care and you're not very tolerant of people who are less precise. You like your surroundings to be just so. You're a very tidy man, Mr Rintoul. You wash up the breakfast things before you go to work.'

'Doesn't everyone?' Linus was surprised.

'I think if you ask around you'll find very few people do, especially if they live alone. At best they rinse things out and leave them to stand—always assuming they have breakfast in the first place.'

'I don't like clutter in the kitchen,' Linus said defensively.

'Or anywhere else, so far as I could see. Books neatly on shelves, magazines in neat piles, briefcase standing neatly beside the settee.'

'You make me sound obsessive,' Linus remarked, alarmed. He was disconcerted by the precision of Netley's observations as much as by the way they sounded when put into words.

'Your choice of words, Mr Rintoul, not mine.'

Linus gathered his damaged self-esteem round him. 'All right, so I'm an old woman—in your opinion. What has that got to do with Huning?'

'You've admitted the phone call frightened you. "Worried" was your word but frightened is what you meant. I think the whole business dented your own self-image and I don't think you liked that. You particularly didn't like the feeling that Huning wasn't letting go that easily. I think you decided to get rid of him—and the threat —once and for all.'

Linus stared at him, aghast. 'You mean you think I pushed him into the Thames?'

'I'm suggesting you had a motive.'

'Hardly an adequate one for murder!'

'You think not? Murder's been done for less, I promise you. It was you who used the word "obsessive", I think.'

'But I was nowhere near the Thames or Maidenhead when he died.'

'How do you know when that was, Mr Rintoul?'

Linus considered. Had it been in the paper? He couldn't remember for sure but rather thought not. 'I don't, I suppose.'

'Then you're hardly in a position to be adamant about it, are you?'

Nettled, Linus flushed. 'As a matter of fact, I am,' he said. 'I know he was alive when we had lunch—and with Lacock as a witness even you can't throw doubt on that. And I know when the report on his body's being found appeared in the paper. It so happens that I've had no call to go anywhere near the Maidenhead area between those days, either professionally—and my time-sheets will tell you where I was—or personally.'

'Ah, but can you prove it? Time-sheets can be pure fiction and I don't suppose you can produce witnesses for every minute of your off-duty hours, now can you?'

Since Linus spent his evenings at home, alone, more often than not, this was an uncomfortably accurate assessment. 'I'm surprised you haven't yet accused me of beating Miriam to death,' he said bitterly.

'There is that, I suppose,' Netley admitted. 'I have to say, though, that I don't think that's quite your style. Too messy.'

They were interrupted at this moment by an apologetic young constable who handed a paper to the unidentified observer and then withdrew.

There was silence in the room while that individual read the communication before handing it to Netley without a word. He, too, read it without comment, then folded it and slipped it into his pocket.

'Now where were we? Ah, yes. Ms Greentree. No, Mr Rintoul, I'd be disinclined to accuse you of that even if we hadn't established your whereabouts to our complete satisfaction. On the other hand, you don't have any great aversion to killing, do you? After all, you are a vet.'

'Sometimes animals have to be put down and it's all part of the job,' Linus replied. 'That doesn't actually make it any easier, you know. I've never met a vet who enjoyed putting them down.'

'No one is suggesting enjoyment, merely a willingness to do it,' Netley pointed out.

'In any case, I don't think you can equate animals with people in this context,' Linus persisted.

'Now there I do agree. I believe you have a shotgun, Mr Rintoul.'

'I'm sure you've found it in the house. It's entirely legal as is the captive-bolt killer which I dare say you've also come across.'

'Quite so. Do you have any other firearms?'

'No.'

'None at all? No hand-gun? No rifle?'

Linus shook his head. 'None.'

'Have you borrowed one recently?'

'Why should I do that?'

'You tell me.'

'I haven't.'

'So it wasn't you who shot your dog?'

Linus flushed with fury. 'That's the most obscene suggestion you've made yet. If I had needed—or wanted—to destroy Ishmael, there are many infinitely less brutal methods at my disposal. I suppose I sent myself that anonymous threat, too?'

'It's been done before.'

'Why should I do such a thing?'

'I'm sure we can find a motive when we've gone into this a bit deeper.'

'I'm sure you can invent one,' Linus retorted. 'That won't make it true.'

Netley glanced up at the third observer and Linus caught the brief assenting nod of the head that was the reply. 'Your dog was killed with a very high powered hand-gun,' Netley went on. 'They've found the bullet which you apparently missed.'

'Where was it?' Linus asked. 'I scrubbed the walls and wiped the carpet down pretty thoroughly, or so I thought. I didn't see anything.'

'Not surprising. It seems to have lodged under the skirting board in a corner, largely hidden by the pile of the carpet. You wouldn't have missed it if you'd been looking for it but it would have been easy enough to overlook otherwise.'

'So why does that make you think I shot him?'

'It doesn't necessarily but there is a strange coincidence. You see, Huning was shot by a very similar weapon.'

'Huning? But he drowned! It said so in the paper!'

'No. It said his body was found in the river—which it was. He had been shot first but it doesn't always suit us to tell the press everything.'

'If his head looked anything like Ishmael's, I should think whoever found him would have mentioned the fact—once they'd stopped throwing up.'

'Why assume he was shot in the head? He wasn't. The dog, of course, could probably hardly have been shot anywhere else since he was presumably barking at whoever had come to the door. Miriam Greentree, on the other hand, probably was.'

Linus was now completely bewildered. 'But I thought her head had been smashed in?'

'It was, but after death. They finally found a heavy calibre bullet lodged in the masonry of the Square Tower and the assumption is that the smashing-in was to disguise the fact that she had been shot.' Netley paused briefly. 'I don't think it's going to surprise anyone if the bullet in your wall proves to be from the same gun.'

'But what possible connection is there between Miriam and Ishmael?'

'Apart from you? Huning, of course. Ms Greentree is an associate of Huning. She is shot, he contacts you and is shot, your dog is shot.'

'Tenuous,' Linus commented.

'Agreed, but rather less so if both bullets are from the same gun. Mr Rintoul, there's something I want you to go away and think about very carefully indeed.'

'Go away? Just like that? You're not keeping me?'

'Not for the moment. We naturally reserve the right to have you in again as our inquiries progress but for the moment you're free to go.'

'Very generous,' Linus said sardonically. 'What is it I've got to think about?'

'I want you to cast your mind back to that phone call. The one you assumed was from Huning. I want you to try everything in your power to remember every single word of it. Don't be put off if it differs from what you've already told us. It's the precise detail we're after. And while you're thinking about it, I want you to ask yourself how certain you are that it really was Huning you spoke to. In other words, if his name had never come up and apparently been accepted by the man at the other end of the line, would you still have believed it was him by the time you finished?'

'Is it so terribly important?'

'We think so.'

CHAPTER 8

By the time the police car dropped Linus at his front door and one of the two accompanying young policemen asked him if he would be all right now, Linus's mind was in a state of total confusion and disorientation. One moment he was merely being helpful, the next he seemed to be under serious suspicion of murder, then he was accused of the unnecessary and brutal killing of his own pet dog and then, with no apparent reason, he was given a great deal of information of a kind he was quite sure the police did not normally volunteer out of the kindness of their hearts, and allowed to go home. It didn't add up. And it hadn't been a pleasant experience. Linus was a truthful man and he didn't like having his word doubted, even though he knew that that was the police's job. Nor was he a violent man, and he found it deeply offensive to be accused of anything as obscene as murder.

Still, he watched a lot of television where interrogation by a 'hard' policeman and then by a 'soft' one was an accepted dramatic strategy. Quite possibly it was also a customary police strategy since one didn't need to be Freud to realize that a mind off-balance is more susceptible to suggestion. Not that Netley had used that technique. Quite the contrary. Neither of the other two policemen had contributed to the questioning at all. All the same, Netley had successfully blown hot, blown cold and the effect on Linus had been the same. He had ended up putting a suggestion in Linus's mind. Linus accepted that if it was necessary for him to consider the speaker's identity, Netley couldn't very well have put it to him any other way. Still, it behoved him to be very, very careful to ensure that if he decided it *was* someone else, he didn't do so because the suggestion had been made when he was confused. By the same token, he must be equally careful that he didn't decide it was Huning just because an officious policeman he didn't much like had suggested otherwise.

Netley's questions about the phone call had served to put Linus's memory in gear and in the course of what was left of the day he was able to go through that conversation in his mind, honing the phrases, rearranging the words, until he was as certain as he could be that when he sat down with the notes he had made, he would be able to assemble them into a version which would be as close to verbatim as it was likely to be after such a time lapse.

He spent the evening writing up the completed conversation and as he did so, he recalled not only the fact that he had assumed it was Huning because he couldn't think who else with an American accent was likely to he phoning him at one o'clock in the morning, but that it hadn't initially sounded like him at all: it had been the content that had really decided it.

Going over the conversation, as he had been, for hours on end, brought that voice very clearly back to mind. Linus could almost hear it, now that he had the phraseology more accurately expressed, and he had serious doubts that is was Huning's. He tried to analyze why. What was it that the voice had—or lacked—that didn't quite fit?

His first impression of Huning had been that he reminded Linus of a Mormon missionary: very clean, very wholesome, very American—and very Ivy League. The voice on the phone had lacked the elusive, cultured Ivy League undertone and there had been something else there instead. Linus racked his brains but was damned if he could pinpoint what it was.

He had done enough to satisfy Netley but he wasn't yet ready to pass on to the detective the results of a hard day's thinking because he knew there was more.

He knew it hadn't been Huning and he knew why but he also knew that the voice had been familiar. Repeatedly going over the conversation reinforced that impression. He could go to Netley, tell him what he knew and leave it at that. Except that he couldn't let it drop. Linus knew that he would go on trying to pin down that elusive memory. In any case, Netley would be sure to say, '. . . and let me know if you remember who it was.' No, Linus would go to him with the full recollection and then he would be able to hand the whole thing over to the police and get back to worrying about ordinary things like Blue Ear Disease, BSE and Rabies.

In practice, work obliged him to push it to the back of his mind for the next few days and he resigned himself to the knowledge that he would have to contact Netley soon with or without that additional piece of information. He didn't do so immediately, however, because it was always hovering just out of reach and knew that sooner or later it would come close enough to be grasped.

It did. In the middle of the night. To be precise, at one o'clock in the morning. Very Freudian, Linus thought. He lay on his back, staring up at the ceiling, darkly grey in the summer night. He went over the conversation again in his mind, putting a new face on the other participant and finding it fitted. It raised a lot of questions, chief among them why the speaker hadn't disabused Linus of his assumption that he was talking to Huning, but that was a matter for Netley to sort out. He'd ring him in the morning.

But Linus didn't. He still intended to while he ate his breakfast but he was having second thoughts by the time he was washing up. Better to be one hundred per cent sure, he told himself. He mentally reviewed the day's programme and smiled to himself. It was ironic that today of all days he should have scheduled a visit to the Maidenhead area. He hadn't been there professionally for months. He'd have plenty of time after he'd visited the small herd of Angora goats. It wouldn't hurt Netley to wait another day.

He had to park some way from the gallery and walk back, but that was no great disadvantage since it meant the car, inconspicuous as it was, wouldn't herald his arrival.

The discus thrower opened the door, his clothes as

carefully casual as ever, with due provision made for the fine summer weather. His pale blue linen slacks were emphatically not jeans and the sleeves of his crisply laundered white shirt were neatly rolled up to halfway along his forearm. His shirt collar was open. It was all very much the young Dirk Bogarde, Linus thought.

'Good morning,' he said.

The discus thrower inclined his head in acknowledgement.

'I wonder if you'd give Mr March a message,' Linus went on.

'He's in the back,' the discus thrower said. 'Why don't you speak to him yourself?'

'Oh, there's no need to take up any of his time. Will you tell him I dropped by to say how very happy I am with the cow.'

The man was momentarily taken aback. 'The cow?'

Linus guessed he had forgotten which picture Linus had bought, or, more probably thought of it by the painter's name rather than by its subject. 'The watercolour I bought. Of a cow.'

Memory refreshed, the man smiled. 'Of course. I'll tell him. Mr March will be pleased.'

'Will be pleased with what?' Raymond March came through the archway from the next display area. 'Ah, Mr . . . Rintoul.' The hesitation was almost imperceptible. It didn't do to forget a customer's name, not even a relatively small customer's. 'How nice to see you again. Can I help you?'

Linus felt rather foolish. One did not customarily pop in just to thank a dealer for having sold one a painting. 'I just came in to say how very happy I am with the painting I bought.'

March looked surprised, as well as might, but gratified.

'I'm glad. Satisfied customers are always a good advertisement. Was that all?'

'Yes. I just happened to be passing. It was a spur of the moment idea. I hope you didn't mind.'

'Not at all,' March murmured. 'Very good of you to bother.'

The discus thrower opened the door and Linus took the hint, satisfied that he had done what he had set out to do. He'd give Netley a ring this afternoon.

He didn't have to. He got back to Oxford around lunchtime and decided to have a quick something at home. Netley, his sergeant and the silent observer of Linus's interview climbed out of an unmarked car.

'Good afternoon, Mr Rintoul,' Netley said affably. 'We're a bit surprised not to have heard from you.'

'As it happens, I was going to ring you this afternoon, but I don't necessarily expect you to believe that,' Linus told him. 'I take it you want to come in?'

'That's very kind of you. We can talk in the car, if you prefer, or we can go along to St Aldate's.'

'Hobson's choice,' Linus commented drily. 'You'll have to watch me eat my lunch, however.' He glanced across at the car as he closed the door behind them. 'I hope you haven't been sitting there long. It seems a dreadful waste of manpower.'

'Not long. Your office didn't expect you back and the girl said it was an even bet you'd drop off at home for a little something. We took a chance.'

Linus handed him the final draft of his revised recollections of the telephone call. 'Here you are, Inspector. It's as accurate as I can make it. And no, it wasn't Huning.'

'How sure of that are you?'

'Absolutely sure.'

'Not influenced by the fact that I put the idea into your head?'

'I took that into account and made allowances for it. Besides, I checked.'

'You went to see Raymond March.' It wasn't a question.

'Either that's a very educated guess or your people have been watching the gallery.'

'Precisely.' Linus noticed that the answer didn't tell him which. 'Mr Rintoul,' Netley went on. 'Don't you think it was rather a foolish thing to do?'

'I'll admit my excuse was a bit lame—I told him I'd popped in to say how happy I was with the picture I bought from him—but foolish?'

Netley sighed. 'Mr Rintoul, a man rings you up telling you, in effect, to mind your own business. Assuming it's Huning, you use that name, thereby indicating someone else involved in whatever it is. Shortly afterwards Huning is found murdered. His associate, Ms Greentree, has already been killed and you have subsequently had your dog shot—and incidentally, the bullet that killed Ishmael and the one that killed Ms Greentree *were* from the same gun. Didn't it strike you as just the teensy-weensiest bit probable that whoever you spoke to might have had something to do with all those deaths? And mightn't that have made your visit to March rather ill-advised?'

He was right, of course, and Linus cursed his insatiable curiosity which impelled him to get to the bottom of things without giving due weight to the possible consequences. He wasn't admitting it to anyone else, however.

'I think the reason I gave was accepted. After all, there's no reason for anyone to think I might have decided the phone call *didn't* come from Huning.'

Netley pursed his lips and nodded reluctantly. 'You may be right. Let's hope so. There are a couple of things still bothering me, though you'll be able to answer at least one of them. Now I've never spoken to March but I've heard he sounds very English.'

'Yes, he does,' Linus said. 'Very.'

'I can understand your assuming an American accent must belong to Huning. I don't know why March should adopt such an accent at all, but I'd also like to know what it was about March's voice that enabled you to see through it.'

Linus stared at him. 'You think it was *March*?'

It was Netley's turn to stare. 'You obviously don't.'

'Good God, no. Nothing like him. It was his minder's voice.'

'His minder? You mean that handsome young assistant?' He turned to his sergeant. 'Refresh my memory, Cote.'

'John Smith. If you remember, sir, we decided that there are people called that and it's about the last name anyone would make up, this side of a naughty weekend in Brighton. We checked him back to a small security firm in . . . Havant.' He looked up. 'Isn't that near Portsmouth, sir?'

'We missed that,' Netley said grimly.

'Before that he was a bouncer in a club in Ryde. Nothing funny about either job.'

'Probably knew March from that one,' Linus suggested. 'Hasn't March got a home on the Isle of Wight?'

'You know about his other home?'

'He told me. It's where the Slovenian Mastiffs are supposed to be. The loot, as well.'

Netley studied him as if he was wondering what other little gems of information Linus was unwittingly party to. 'So it was John Smith. What was it about his voice that was familiar?'

'I don't know why I didn't pick it up straight away,' Linus told him. 'I noticed it the only time I heard him speak. He's not what you might call garrulous, you know. I suppose it was the time of night combined with the American edge. John Smith had an American accent, all right, but it's that rather odd accent that Europeans acquire when they've learnt their English in America or been taught by Americans. The first time I heard him, I tried to place the European undertones and failed. I wasn't any more successful today but it was the same voice. There's no question about that.'

The hitherto silent one of the three spoke for the first time. 'My name's Kirkstall, Mr Rintoul. Now I don't want to put ideas into your head so think carefully before you answer. Do you think those European undertones might have been German?'

Linus considered. There was a very slight problem with 'th' which might have been an impediment but then again, might not. More specifically, now he started to analyze it, he realized that the undertone lay in the way the man used his mouth which in turn affected the sounds that came out. Germans do not make extensive use of their lips as, say, Italians do; in particular they tend not to push them forward. On the other hand they do extend their mouths sideways so that 'have', for example, emerges as 'hev'.

'I'd say German was his first language,' he said at last. 'He could be Austrian—or Swiss—I suppose. I'll leave that to you.'

'Perhaps Sergeant Cote can make use of your telephone again, Mr Rintoul,' Netley said.

Linus grinned. 'To get a more thorough check done on Mr Smith? Feel free.' He got the distinct impression that his little pleasantry wasn't altogether appreciated. It was nice to hit a nerve sometimes, especially a nerve of someone who made a profession of doing it himself.

Netley leaned back in his armchair with the air of one who is settling himself in for a good, long visit. 'Well, now, Mr Rintoul, you're an intelligent man and not at all bad at putting two and two together. What do you make of all this?'

Linus looked at him suspiciously. 'Isn't that your job?'

'Yes, and I'm probably a lot better at it than you, but sometimes it's illuminating to have a completely fresh opinion. Out of the mouths, and all that.'

'I see. And am I rated a babe or a suckling?'

Netley chuckled. He sounded almost human, Linus thought. 'More the elementary science student,' he said.

Linus smiled reluctantly. It was all too easy to underestimate Detective-Inspector Netley. He suspected that might well be one of the policeman's most useful weapons. He sat in silence for some time, not because he had much doubt about what two and two added up to in this case, but because he needed to marshall his thoughts into a coherent sequence.

'I don't think it's too complex,' he said at last, cautiously. 'Raymond March is an ex-Nazi who either stole or helped hide (and quite probably both) Nazi loot. He says he's only sixty-five, which would make him improbably young at the time, but—'

'Hang on a minute,' Netley interrupted. 'When did he tell you his age—and why, for God's sake?'

Linus looked mildly surprised. 'He didn't. He told the Kennel Club.'

'The Kennel Club? Where do they come in all this? You haven't mentioned them before.'

'Because they're not really germane to the story; they're purely peripheral. He was standing for the General Committee, you see, and you can't serve over the age of seventy-five. Now, no one says he was that old, but several members were of the opinion he'd had plastic surgery to make himself look younger.'

'Bit drastic,' Kirkstall commented. 'Is the General Committee that important?'

'I don't think they thought that. Just that he was rather vain. But if he had plans to cash in on the loot, it would help to look too young to have had anything to do with the stealing of it, don't you think? And the rewards would certainly make the surgery worth while.'

'A fresh eye on it, indeed,' Netley murmured.

'He has a gallery—an ideal outlet, though in my opinion a bit too obvious,' Linus went on. 'He also has a false floor in the transit he uses for the dogs, which would be ideal for transporting pictures you wished to keep quiet.'

He had the satisfaction of seeing that this was news to Netley, who whistled through his teeth. 'Has he, by God?'

'He has a very isolated home which he described to me as being in the Solent, by which I take it he means on the north coast of the Isle of Wight.' He paused as a thought struck him. 'Now why did I assume that? It could equally well be on the mainland coast. Anyway, that's where the treasures are stored or, perhaps more probably, where they're brought to prior to being sold to certain carefully selected collectors. He's a wealthy man by any criteria and he must have had a succession of minders, security guards, personal assistants, call them what you will. It would obviously be an advantage if they themselves had Nazi leanings.'

Kirkstall's eyes narrowed and he leaned forward. 'Have you any reason to believe John Smith has such a leaning?' he asked.

'I've never given it much thought,' Linus said. 'So I suppose the answer's no. Wait a minute, though. Maybe. The one thing that mars that Adonis beauty is a long, thin scar on one cheek. Aren't duelling scars a sort of badge of honour among Nazis?'

'They certainly used to be,' Kirkstall agreed. 'But duelling's been illegal there since the war for that very reason and he's too young to have acquired them before.'

'I don't see what illegality's got to do with it,' Linus said after a little thought. 'I mean, cock-fighting, dog-fighting and bare-knuckle pugilism have all been illegal here since goodness knows when, but they go on just the same. Only dog-fighting ever actually stopped—if it did,' he added cynically. 'It doesn't take much skill to mend a clean slash and if a doctor—or a vet, for that matter—happens to be a Nazi sympathizer (and there must be some), then both the skill and the antibiotics are there.'

'Point taken,' Kirkstall conceded.

'Anyway,' Linus went on, 'that's the set-up as I see it. How much about his business any minder would need to know, I'm not sure. Maybe he only needs to be willing to do as he's told, no matter what. On the other side we have Miriam and Huning and, presumably, other associates, but certainly backers. They may be interested in returning the art to its original owners, but I doubt it. My guess is they tracked it to March and were solely interested in acquiring it for themselves, either to sell or because their backers are collectors, in which case there'd be a nice fat fee in it for them.'

'Go on.'

Linus warmed to his theme. 'When the minder saw Miriam with me at the dog show, he certainly recognized her. Maybe he'd seen her watching the gallery or maybe he knew her from somewhere else, I don't know, but she was killed soon afterwards. My guess is by him, though whether on March's orders or off his own bat, I leave to you to decide. Maybe they were following me after that. I wasn't aware of it, but then, I had no reason to expect it. If they were, they saw me go into the pub and they'd have seen Huning come out. Now they certainly weren't inside the pub because it was empty except—later—for Inspector Lacock. They'd have had no way of knowing whether we were three individuals with no connection with each other or whether we were all meeting by prior arrangement, but if they knew Huning, they'd have needed to find out whether there was a connection. Hence the phone call during which I gave Huning's name, thus telling them I knew him. We know what happened to him.' Linus looked round at his audience. 'All right so far?'

'Apart from the what-ifs and the maybes,' Netley said. 'It's certainly interesting. Do go on.'

Linus felt understandably inhibited by this comment. 'There isn't much more,' he said. 'They killed Ishmael and sent me a warning note to frighten me off and that's about it.'

'Why not just kill you instead?'

'Why bother? I'm only on the sidelines and the more individuals who're murdered, the more likely your lot are to find enough evidence to track the murderer down.'

'That's certainly very true,' Cote commented.

Linus looked from one to the other. 'Well?' he asked. 'How does it strike you? It fits the facts.'

'And makes up quite a few of them as it goes along,' Netley said.

'I'll agree there's a bit of theorizing,' Linus said defensively. 'But surely you must theorize from time to time?'

'Oh, we do. Quite often. In some cases that's all we've got. But we stick to one hard and fast rule.'

'Which is?'

'We first make sure such facts as we have are proven facts.'

'And mine aren't?'

'Mr Rintoul, your version of events is both intelligent and plausible, given your assumption of the facts. Unfortunately it's also based on one hugely inaccurate premise.'

'Which is?' Linus asked again.

'There is no such thing as a hidden cache of stolen masterpieces. Or, if there is, Raymond March has—and had—nothing whatever to do with it and neither did Greentree and Huning. It's back to the drawing-board, I'm afraid.'

CHAPTER 9

When the door had closed behind them, Linus felt a complete and utter prat. He blushed with shame. How could he have been such a fool? His folly had not lain so much in believing the yarn about a hoard of Nazi loot, though that was daft enough, but in so earnestly putting forward his considered explanation of recent events. Netley and his colleagues had sat there, po-faced, apparently taking him as seriously as he demonstrably took himself and all the time they must have been laughing at him up their sleeves. That was what really hurt. Linus had a very sharp sense of humour and he had no objection to being laughed at provided he was in on the joke, but he wasn't sufficiently self-assured to face with equanimity, much less with a smile, the fact that others were laughing at him behind his back.

Inside he felt ready to curl up and die. He now knew exactly how a wounded animal feels when it hides itself away until time either kills or cures. There were only two small consolations. One was that only he and the three policemen knew about it, though he doubted whether they would be able to keep it to themselves for long: it was a story that begged to be told. The other was that he wouldn't have to see them ever again. And even that would be too soon.

Why had they led him on to make such a fool of himself? Had it been out of sheer malice? A sort of psychological sadism? Linus didn't like Netley but he wouldn't have put him down as a malicious man, and Linus knew he wasn't *that* bad a judge of character. Perhaps Netley had been getting his own back for Linus's earlier pedantry? That was possible and certainly more likely. Or perhaps by encouraging him to make such a fool of himself, they simply ensured that henceforth he kept his nose well and truly out of the March affair. Or was is the Greentree–Huning affair? With the destruction of the loot scenario, it was quite likely that Raymond March didn't come into it at all.

His minder did, though. John Smith. The voice on the telephone had been his. Maybe all it was was a simple plot to rob a very wealthy are dealer of all his stock. Maybe John Smith was—what was the expression?—in cahoots with Greentree and Huning originally and there had been a falling-out among thieves. Maybe . . .

Enough! Linus pulled himself up short. Haven't your stupid speculations brought you enough trouble already? Leave it. Whatever's going on, it's not your business, it's the police's. Let them handle it. Drop it. Back off. Back right away, in fact, and get on with the job you're paid to do by an insufficiently grateful British government.

In the ensuing days, Linus found it wasn't always easy to follow his own advice and he not infrequently found speculation niggling at the corners of his mind. He found the instant remedy lay in reminding himself of the conclusion of that last interview. He had almost stopped blushing when he thought of it, but he still shuddered.

Another revelation had come out of his talks with Netley and it rankled with a severity that increased as his speculation on past events diminished. He went over to the quarantine kennels and, with the liberty accorded to old friends, left David Thelwall dealing with some minor veterinary matter and went into the kitchen to beg a cup of coffee from Ruth.

'Can I ask you something?' he asked, studiously stirring the milk round in his mug.

'Of course you can,' she said, adding lightly, 'Provided I can reserve the right not to answer.'

'No answer would be just as informative, as a matter of fact.'

'Oh, dear. Maybe you'd better not ask, then.'

'If you can't ask your friends, who can you ask?'

'Linus, this is sounding more and more ominous. It's beginning to sound like the sort of question to which people insist they want a truthful answer and yet to which a truthful answer may spell the end of a beautiful friendship.'

Linus thought about that. 'Yes,' he said. 'I'm afraid it's exactly that sort of question.'

'Then take my advice and don't ask it,' Ruth said briskly.

'I think I have to. Ruth, in your opinion—your honest opinion—am I an old woman?'

She looked at him, briefly surprised, and then laughed. 'No, Linus, that isn't the phrase that springs to mind.'

'Are you sure? You're not just saying that to be kind?'

Ruth sighed. 'See what I mean? I've told you the truth and now you don't want to believe it. What brought all this on?'

'Something someone said.'

'They used that expression? They called you an old woman?'

'No, not in so many words. It's just that . . . well, I was brought up to be neat and tidy and, on the whole, I am. I'm fussy about words, too, and they commented on that. It added up to an old woman.'

Ruth reached across the breakfast bar and laid her hand on his. 'Linus, scientists are a bit like solicitors: they do tend to be precise in their use of language and to be irritated by imprecision. Some of them don't extend that beyond their specialism, especially the younger ones who very often haven't had a very good general education, who have only the minimum language qualification needed to get them into University and little or no interest in the cultural world beyond their discipline. You don't come into that deprived category, thank God. Yes, you're inclined to be pedantic, but so what? As to your being tidy—how tidy? I mean, if you have visitors, do you make them take their shoes off? Do you empty the ashtrays while they're still using them? Do you plump up the cushions when they've popped off to the loo?'

Linus stared at her in horror. 'Good God, no!'

'Then you're not an old woman.'

He stared at her, fascinated. 'Are you telling me there really are people who do that sort of thing?'

'Lots. Mostly women and usually women who've never had any children. Children tend to put the kybosh on that degree of house-pride. Very occasionally you find men like it, and they've usually been only children brought up by a doting and widowed mother—or by parents who had them in middle age. Does that fit you?'

'No. My mother made us put things away and clean our shoes before we went to bed, that sort of thing, and when we complained, she said it was because she was born lazy and saw no reason to do for us things we were perfectly capable of doing for ourselves.'

'Sounds reasonable to me.'

'My wife found it irritating.'

'I don't want to be rude, Linus, but by all accounts your wife was very rarely satisfied. If you'd been the reverse, she'd have grumbled about that. If you'd provided her with a stately home, fully staffed, and a title, she might have been content, but it wouldn't have lasted. She was always after the grass in the next field, even if it was likely to give her bloat.'

Linus chuckled. It was a very accurate picture. 'So you don't think I need worry?' he persisted.

Ruth studied him consideringly. 'No, not yet. I think, in fifteen or twenty years, you *could* turn into an old woman if you aren't careful but the cure's quite simple.'

'I'm almost afraid to ask. What is it?'

'Find yourself another woman.'

'Easier said than done.'

'Rubbish. You're an attractive man, though I don't think you know it—and that makes a nice change, I can tell you.'

'Women I get associated with seem to meet untimely ends,' Linus said. 'It does rather put one off trying.'

'Perhaps you should lower your sights,' Ruth suggested. 'You do rather go for high-fliers, you know. You could do worse than think about it.'

David came into the kitchen then and the conversation turned naturally and without any difficult hiatus into veterinary channels. Linus had been a bit afraid she'd extend the previous subject to include David and he was glad she had enough tact not even to mention it. Very likely she would do, later, when they were alone, but he wouldn't know about that. He left the house feeling a great deal happier. He didn't think Ruth had been merely telling him what she thought he wanted to hear—and he didn't think that conclusion could be attributed to wishful thinking.

Over the next ten days, Linus almost succeeded in putting the whole business out of his mind. That is to say, he didn't think about it above two or three times a day and sometimes did the crossword in the local paper before he remembered to comb its pages for any small reference to someone's being arrested. He still cringed at the recollection of the fool he had made himself, but Ruth's reassurances had gone a long way towards restoring his self-esteem. He gave a lot more thought to her advice than she probably anticipated when she gave it.

She was right about a woman. He'd been on his own for several years now and although he flattered himself that he had come to terms quite well with being alone, there was no denying the fact that a woman about the place would be a distinct improvement. The right woman, that is. He supposed it was quite flattering to be told the women he went out with were—what was Ruth's phrase?—high-fliers. Thinking about it, he supposed they were. He wasn't really drawn to the other sort. He never had been. Even his wife had been a cut above the average which, in view of the end result of that marriage, was a pretty good endorsement of Ruth's advice to lower his sights. The truth was that what would suit him best was a nice, sensible, farmer's daughter—like Ruth. Unfortunately, what would suit him best and what he actually wanted had not yet manifested themselves in one woman—or at least, not in any woman that had so far come Linus's way. The other sort, Ruth's 'high-fliers', were thin on the ground at the best of times and were mostly already spoken for and, as he knew to his cost, those that weren't were not infrequently mixed up in what his mother would have called hanky-panky—a phrase which on her lips had no sexual connotations. It was said there were women who dreamed of a knight on a white charger and preferred remaining single to settling for anything less. His mental image was of a thirty-five-year-old Audrey Hepburn or Sophia Loren, though he was prepared not to be dogmatic about the thirty-five. Maybe a vision of the unattainable and an unwillingness to compromise was a subconscious way of not risking a second marriage failure. Still, it would do no harm to bear Ruth's words in mind. He could at the very least look at women from that point of view, if only as an academic exercise.

It was an academic exercise that certainly brightened up his lunches in pubs scattered around the county, even if the results were not quite what Ruth would have hoped for. He came back from one such lunch in high good humour. It had been market day, the pub had been full and every one of them had been a distinctly low-flier, leaving his sexual appetite comfortably unaroused, but he had heard several disconnected snippets of conversation of the sort that tantalize the imagination and they alone had been worth the lunch.

With nothing more to do that afternoon except get his paperwork up to date, he drove with no undue haste back to Government Buildings. When he stuck his head in the door to tell Lisa he was in, a burly six-foot cloud in the shape of Detective-Sergeant Cote effectively chilled his mood simply by being there.

'Someone to see you,' Lisa said.

'So I gather. You'd better come into my office, Sergeant.' Linus led the way across the sloping corridor and ushered the policeman in. 'I thought I'd seen the last of you,' he said. 'What do you want this time?'

'Detective-Inspector Netley wondered if you'd be kind enough to accompany me to St Aldate's.'

'Do I have a choice?'

Cote looked surprised. 'Of course you do, sir. But Inspector Netley would be obliged.'

'I bet he would,' Linus said with unwonted savagery and resisted the temptation to inquire whether they were short of a laugh or two at the station. 'Does this come under the heading of Helping the Police with their Inquiries?'

'I suppose it does, in a manner of speaking.' The policeman allowed himself a broad grin. 'We don't often invite people with a view to *hindering* them.'

'What I mean is, whether this is likely to be a long visit?'

'Is it important, sir?'

'Oddly enough, it is. I don't object to giving up the government's time; I strongly object to giving up my own.'

'In my job, I find it always pays to anticipate the worst.'

'Thank you very much, Sergeant. That puts my mind completely at ease.'

'We aim to please,' Cote said, grinning appreciatively as he held the door open for Linus.

Linus glanced at him as he passed. 'Does your boss know you've got this sense of humour?' he asked.

'As to that, I'm sure I couldn't say, sir. Not much call for it in the normal course of events.'

Linus was shown into a room which bore no resemblance to the spartan emptiness of the interview room he had been in before. Netley and Kirkstall were there, together with a man who was introduced to Linus as Chief Superintendent Woburn of the Hampshire Constabulary. There was also another plain clothes officer whose name was not given but who appeared to be Kirkstall's sidekick.

Linus was given a chair, one with a padded seat and back, he noted, and wondered whether this rated honourable guest status.

'Coffee, Mr Rintoul?'

Definitely honoured guest, Linus decided, accepting. Either that, or they're softening me up for something.

'You've been very helpful in the past, Mr Rintoul,' Netley went on, 'and we're hoping you'll be so again.'

'Balls!' Linus said crudely. 'All I did before was to make a complete fool of myself—and you led me into it.'

'You were on the wrong tack but in the course of expounding your theory, you filled in one or two little gaps. Like the Kennel Club.'

'The Kennel Club? But that was incidental. Oh, it was perhaps what sparked off my interest in March, in a way, but that's all.'

'Not at all. We knew someone was trying to trace March's birth certificate; we discovered it was a high-powered firm of solicitors and—with great difficulty, I may say—we found out on whose behalf they were working. But we didn't know why and we couldn't imagine why. That bothered us. You solved that one and, as it happens, you're quite right: if that's the reason they want to know, it doesn't matter.' He paused and looked at Linus thoughtfully. 'Mr

Rintoul, I take it you are familiar with the Official Secrets Act?'

Linus was clearly taken aback. 'I've heard of it—and as a government employee, I'm subject to it. I've never read it, though, so I wouldn't say I was familiar with it.'

Netley gave one of his thin smiles. 'Just reminding you,' he said. 'None of what you may learn is to be passed on, not even to your friends in the Kennel Club, not even to a fellow-Mason.'

'I'm no Mason,' Linus said indignantly. 'And I'm not a member of the Kennel Club.'

'Good, then there'll be no conflict of interest on either count, will there?'

Linus was intrigued, as he guessed he was meant to be. He was also apprehensive. Although, like all civil servants —indeed, like all citizens, if it came to the crunch—he was subject to the Official Secrets Act, he might just as well not have been for all the difference it had ever made to him. He did not, for instance, think twice about telling the woman in the corner shop that the chocolate digestives were for the MAFF offices even though several years ago a newspaper had revealed that even such innocuous information was supposed to be kept strictly under wraps. Now his attention had been drawn to this which was, at the very least, an indication that he was getting into territory which might well prove heavy going. He looked Netley straight in the eye.

'I think we've reached the point where I ask to go home,' he said.

'Oh, come, Mr Rintoul. Where's your sense of adventure?'

'It's just died.'

'Aren't you the least bit curious?'

Linus gave that some consideration. 'Yes, I'm curious but I'm not *that* curious. Curiosity in the past has got me into some moderately unpleasant situations. They do say one should learn from experience. The voice of my experience tells me to go home. Now.'

'If you insist, we can't keep you but I have to tell you we'd be very sorry indeed if you did. We need your help. If we didn't, we wouldn't have asked you here. Believe me, we'd rather work without outside help.'

'Is it just professional advice you're after, or something more concrete?'

'Something quite a bit more concrete.'

'I like it less and less. I assume it's dangerous?'

'Crossing the road is dangerous, Mr Rintoul. Especially in Oxford. I'd say that what we'd like you to do for us is considerably less risky than driving down Cowley Road in the rush hour.'

'Fine—and am I supposed to jump at it on that basis?'

'Not at all. I reminded you of the Official Secrets Act because we've already agreed that, before we ask for your commitment, we have to tell you what it's all about. I can reassure you that we wouldn't be doing so if we had the slightest suspicion that your involvement in events so far was anything other than accidental. What you must understand, however, is that if you breathe one single, solitary word of what we tell you, outside these walls—No, if you so much as breathe the merest ghost of a hint that you know anything about it—you can expect to be clapped up inside forthwith. If you're lucky.'

'And if I'm not lucky?'

'The trouble with court cases is the publicity they attract. A nasty accident would prevent a court case. If it happened early enough, it would even pre-empt charges.'

'I didn't think you people were allowed to make threats,' Linus said, unsure how seriously to take Netley's remarks.

'Who's making threats? If you break the Official Secrets Act, you go to gaol. That's the law. The rest, if you think about it, was simply a statement of fact. Are you a gabber, Mr Rintoul?'

Linus thought about it. 'No, I don't think I am.'

'Good, so you've nothing to worry about. At least let me fill you in.'

'OK, I'll listen—but please no promises, mind.'

'Fair enough.' Netley glanced across at Kirkstall who gave another of his barely perceptible nods. Not for the first time, Linus judged that, while Netley might be the mouthpiece, it was Kirkstall who was pulling the strings, and nothing about Kirkstall had been explained except his name.

'You weren't entirely wrong about March,' Netley went on. 'He was born a German and he was a Nazi. The whole works: from Hitler Youth to SS. Our Mr March was not a nice man at all.'

'What was his original name?' Linus asked.

This time Kirkstall infinitesimally shook his head.

'That's not germane to the story,' Netley told him. 'But you were right about his age. He's actually seventy-three but if your friends at the Kennel Club had asked him for a copy of his birth certificate, it would have said he was sixty-five, or so I'm credibly informed.'

'A forgery?'

'I haven't seen it, so I couldn't say. To tell you the truth, no one in this room has seen it. I only know that he has one and if it is a forgery, I'm reasonably confident it would be beyond the powers of the Kennel Club to prove it.'

'As a matter of curiosity, would this birth certificate be —or purport to be—a British one?' Linus asked.

'I believe it may be. Your friends at the Kennel Club raised the possibility of plastic surgery and your own, admittedly inexpert, observations endorsed this suspicion. You're quite right. The purpose was two-fold: it made certain fairly considerable structural changes to his face and it ensured that as he aged, his appearance didn't conflict with the age on his birth certificate. That aspect of it has needed attention from time to time, but he's a very rich man so he took care of that himself.'

'From which I infer that someone else took care of the initial, more major, surgery.'

'Sometimes, Mr Rintoul, I find you uncomfortably acute. Yes. The British Government.'

'If Raymond March was a member of the SS and, in your words, not a very nice man—a description I take, with respect, to be a typically British understatement—why should the British government help him change his face, acquire a false birth certificate and—presumably—set him up in business here? Why wasn't he simply hanged?'

'That's a very loaded question, Mr Rintoul, and preceded by some rather sweeping assumptions.'

'I don't think so. If he needed to change his appearance that drastically, he was running away from something pretty awful. I'd run away from hanging, if I could. So would you. And what Germans got hanged for at the end of the War was war crimes. You've already said he was in the SS. It's not too far-fetched to assume he'd committed his share of atrocities. So why not hang him? After a trial, of course,' Linus added magnanimously.

'Let's leave Raymond March for a while,' Netley said, deliberately not commenting on Linus's deductions. 'I'd like to turn to Miriam Greentree and David Huning. They knew at least as much about March as I've just told you and very likely a whole lot more. You assumed they were working for others. You were right. They were. You also assumed they were up to no good. March would certainly agree with that and so would the official view. Individuals might well have reservations. They were certainly operating in a grey area of the law. They may or may not already have been in contravention of the all-embracing Official

Secrets Act but what was more important was what they did with anything they found out. I believe there was a watch of sorts being kept on them—but not closely enough, it would seem. They were professional Nazi-hunters, Mr Rintoul. David Huning, his all-American-college-boy appearance notwithstanding, was an American-educated Israeli and we suspect he was a Mossad agent as well. You've heard of Mossad? The Israeli secret police?'

Linus nodded. 'I've heard of them.'

'Miriam Greentree was an English-born Jew. Her parents fled here before the war. They were the only members of what had been a very large family to survive the holocaust.'

'She told me that.'

'What she didn't tell you was that she had volunteered to help track down any ex-Nazis who might be in Britain.'

'Are there many? I wouldn't have thought it was a safe place in which to seek refuge.'

'We don't think so, but we know of some. The Nazi-hunters, as you no doubt know, track down Nazis accused of atrocities and in particular of those perpetrated against Jews. They assemble the evidence which, of course, includes finding reliable witnesses, and get the accused brought to trial, if necessary by getting such people to a country which is prepared to try them after all this time.'

'Smuggling them out, you mean.'

'They'd hardly go willingly.'

'It sounds a perfectly laudable aim to me,' Linus commented. 'In fact, I'd only have reservations if they got someone out of the country by underhand means. I take it they were after March.'

'That's right.'

'With justification?'

'With very considerable justification.'

'I thought Parliament had just passed a law allowing war

criminals to be prosecuted here? There was a lot of fuss about it at the time and I seem to recall that the Lords threw it out but it went through just the same. Or didn't it?'

'It went through.'

'So that wasn't a problem. All they had to do was to present their evidence to the appropriate authorities here, and the case would take its course.' Netley said nothing, a fact which made Linus look at him rather more sharply. The detective seemed to be waiting for something. 'Hang on a minute,' Linus went on. 'You already knew all this. Or did you? Had the Greentree–Huning partnership given you the information on March?'

'They hadn't come near us.'

'So you knew anyway?'

'We always had known.'

'Then why hadn't you already acted? Why didn't you arrest him as soon as the Act became law?'

'I thought you'd get there in the end,' Netley said, glancing at Kirkstall with some satisfaction. 'As it happens, you've put your finger on the nub of our problem—and I'll tell you this, Rintoul, I don't like what I'm going to tell you any more than I imagine you'll like hearing it.'

Linus noted the unconscious dropping of the previous punctiliously formal use of his title. If 'sides' were being taken, Netley had lined himself up with Linus, psychologically, if nothing else. 'Go on,' he said.

'It appears that at the end of the war, when it became clear that something very nasty was going to happen to a lot of people who deserved something a hell of a lot worse, the charming Mr March, who had not only been unpleasantly active himself in no fewer than three concentration camps in the course of the war, had also kept very detailed records, in the form of a diary, relating to the activities of his colleagues. "Diary" is a bit of a misnomer, because the one thing he took very good care not to record was anything at all that specifically mentioned himself. He didn't even record what he had for dinner. The reason for this was, apparently, that he didn't altogether believe in the Thousand-Year Reich and he could foresee a time when it might be to his advantage to be able to blackmail some people in very high positions who might prefer their earlier professional careers to be, if not forgotten, at least not recalled in too much detail. It didn't work out quite as he planned, of course, but Mr March is nothing if not an opportunist and he very quickly realized that those diaries were his way out of the noose. He traded in his diary for immunity from prosecution, a new identity and a new life.'

'A truly charming man,' Linus commented. 'Why didn't the authorities take the diary and charge him just the same?'

Netley shook his head and tut-tutted. 'Dear me, whatever happened to gentlemanly conduct and word of honour? No, nasty as he was, March was always a relatively small fish in a very murky pond, but his diary provided evidence against some very big fish indeed. The government of the day judged it to be a thoroughly advantageous deal. Enter Raymond March with a new nose, an altered jaw-line and amended cheek-bones. Plus a nice new birth certificate and an undertaking that so long as he remained on British soil, we would discreetly protect him.'

'Does that mean that he's had a police guard for the last forty years at the taxpayer's expense?' Linus asked, horrified.

'Even our misguided generosity doesn't run to that,' Netley assured him. 'But if he thinks something's wrong, we come running. We knew the Greentree woman was watching him and we soon checked her out. Unfortunately, there wasn't much we could do about her. We couldn't warn her off as March would have liked, because we were sure she was looking for evidence rather than had found it, and anything we said would be a clear indication she was on the right tack.'

'So you got rid of her.'

'No. The police certainly had nothing to do with it and I'm assured that no other branch of the security services had, either.'

'Hm.' Linus was sceptical. 'They would say that, wouldn't they?'

Kirkstall intervened briefly. 'They would, indeed, Mr Rintoul. I can only assure you that on this occasion they didn't, any more than they shot your dog—which was done with the same gun.'

'If that's true—and I'm far from convinced—it suggests it must have been done by March because it looked to him as if you weren't doing enough to protect him. Huning too, I suppose.'

'So far we have nothing concrete to link the murder of Huning with the other two killings, other than the coincidence of his being Greentree's colleague,' Netley reminded him.

'A not inconsiderable coincidence, given the circumstances,' Linus suggested.

'Agreed, but not enough for a jury. It also seems improbable that March himself would have done it. His track record is for keeping his nose clean and the one weapon he would be the least likely to use would be one issued to the German military during the war, which is what we think was used.'

'You can tell that from the bullets?'

'No, but we can hazard an educated guess from the cartridge cases. One was found in the shingle on Portsmouth beach which by a stroke of sheer good fortune hadn't been dragged out to sea with the swash. We've hunted for the one that killed your dog, but unfortunately, you don't have a front garden and either it was picked up by some schoolboy or it landed in the gutter and from there into the sewers. Pity, that. I like these things to fit together neatly. We don't know for sure what kind of gun it was but among the probabilities is a Walther P.38. Does that mean anything to you?'

'Not a thing.'

'Pity. It's fairly unusual in this country, and since you may well encounter it in the course of what we hope you're going to do for us, it would help. Do you know the difference between a semi-automatic and a revolver?'

'To look at, you mean? Yes—I watch television as much as the next man.'

'Good. It's a semi-automatic. Keep your eyes open.'

'Look, I don't want you to think I'm being obstructive, or anything,' Linus said, 'but this talk of automatics doesn't quite tie in with the absence of risk you promised me.'

'I don't think I said anything about an *absence* of risk, Rintoul. I may have said there was *less* risk than crossing the road. Not the same thing at all. Guns have been known to miss, you know.'

'Not this one, by all accounts,' Linus said drily. 'And I suppose if March is ruled out as the actual murderer, we're looking at John Smith. Now there's a young man who strikes me as remarkably well coordinated. I think I'd rather have March's seventy-three-year-old eyes on the target than young Adonis's, especially if I happen to be the target.'

'We hope to have you away before we get that far,' Netley reassured him. 'How well did you know those dogs of his —the ones in quarantine?'

'Not very. I examined them two or three times. That's all.'

'Any problem?'

'None at all. Nor were they a problem to the young vet

who inspected the kennels before I did. Thelwall found them straight-forward enough.'

'That's not what our research suggests,' Netley told him. 'Our dog-handlers say they're a very nasty breed indeed.'

'Do they, indeed? And what the hell do your dog-handlers know about it?' Linus retorted, irritated by the blanket condemnation. 'The breed isn't in any reference book, it isn't recognized by the Kennel Club in its country of origin and our Kennel Club couldn't find out anything about it, either. So where have your men got their information from?'

'They take the view that any Central European mastiff-type dog is going to be a liability. In fact, they're suggesting it should become a prohibited breed.'

'Interesting legal problem, there,' Linus said. 'How do you prohibit a breed when there's no concrete evidence that there *is* such a breed? And is this what we can look forward to now—the banning of any dog on the say-so of some moron who *thinks* it *might* be dangerous? Why, your handlers can't even have seen the damned things.'

'That's where you're wrong. One of them overflew the property in a chopper. He saw the dogs and wasn't happy.'

'My heart bleeds,' Linus snorted. 'I was under the impression March's other house—which I presume is where he saw them—was both isolated and virtually escape-proof in dog terms.'

'Oh, it is.'

'So what's all this about? March is a member of the Kennel Club. He's unlikely to be irresponsible about his dogs no matter how unpleasant he may be in other respects.'

'So the dogs don't worry you?'

'No, but then, I've met them.'

'Good. So you won't mind meeting them again.'

Linus sat back in his chair and laughed. 'Ah, so at last we're getting there. What have you in mind?'

'Your verbal precision has let you down in one respect, Rintoul. You said that you'd been told March had a place in the Solent and you assumed that meant on the Isle of Wight, even though that would surely have been referred to as being "on" the Solent. "In" is the correct word. March's other home is very definitely "in" the Solent. You visited Portsmouth. Didn't your stay take you along the sea-front?'

'Of course it did. Several times.'

It was Chief Superintendent Woburn's time to join in the questioning. 'Didn't you happen to notice some very large, circular, stone blockhouses at intervals across the channel?'

'You mean the Spithead forts? Yes. I went over one of them.'

'That'll be Spit Bank. Good. You've made our job a lot easier, Mr Rintoul.'

'Hang on a minute,' Linus said. He remembered his dream that, given enough money and the right architect, Spit Bank would convert into a rather unusual home. Raymond March had the money and the right taste to choose an appropriate architect. Envy was not an emotion that often afflicted Linus, but it came close to doing so now. 'Do you mean March's home is one of those forts?'

'That's right. Horse Sand.'

'And where do I come into all this?' At the back of Linus's mind was the thought that he wouldn't be at all averse to seeing what March had done with his basic material.

Kirkstall re-entered the conversation. 'We're bound to protect March,' he said. 'But that doesn't entitle the man to break the law. He's not immune from prosecution on any count other than war crimes. Now someone killed Greentree and Huning. It's more likely to be this so-called John Smith —about whom, I'm ashamed to say, we've been able to dig up virtually nothing, an alarming enough circumstance in itself—than March himself, but if it's one of them, and they have a gun—for which neither has a firearms certificate—we need to get on that fort and search, and we don't labour under the illusion that we're going to be welcome.'

'Presumably you can arm yourselves with a search warrant,' Linus said with the authority of a man who watches television.

'And one or two other things besides,' Kirkstall told him. 'If you've been over Spit Bank, you know there are only two ways of reaching one of those forts: by sea or by chopper—and Horse Sand has a helipad. We know we're dealing with dangerous men and, in March's case, with a very nervous one: as soon as that Act was passed, he was very anxious to find out if it affected his position in any way.'

'Understandable,' Linus commented.

'Very,' Kirkstall agreed. 'It's bound to make him edgy, though. Now a helicopter landing is easily taken out by a good shot and anyone who sets foot on the top of the fort has to contend with those two dogs. We reckon an approach by sea will be easier to pull off unobserved if we use an unmarked boat and personnel in plain clothes because those waters are bursting at the seams with craft of one sort or another and very often they circle the forts out of sheer curiosity. We'll be seen but not noticed until the very last moment. If we're really lucky we may even get one or two men on to the landing-stage unobserved. It's the dogs that are the problem.'

'Which is where I come in, I take it,' Linus said.

'Exactly. We can shoot them, of course, but that would draw as much attention to ourselves as the dogs' barking. On the other hand, you know them and they know you. We want you to lure them to you and slip them something to knock them out, thus eliminating one hazard.'

'Wouldn't it be easier to use a local vet? Perhaps whoever looks after the Hampshire Constabulary's dogs, or those belonging to Customs and Excise?'

'We considered that. You'll be better. For one thing, like I said, they know you. For another, you're a full-time government employee and have already signed the Act which saves us having to make a big drama out of it with someone who hasn't. And lastly, not only do you know these dogs, but you're not afraid of them. That helps!'

Linus had to agree. There were a lot of vets in private practice these days who were quite frankly scared of dogs, especially big ones, and who muzzled or taped any dog needing treatment, a policy that had ruined the temperament of many dogs who wouldn't previously have dreamed of threatening a vet, much less biting one. All too many of his profession these days were scientists first and animal handlers a long way last. He sighed.

'So there I am with my head stuck over the parapet whispering, "Good doggie, come here, doggie, have a chockie-drop, doggie," in the knowledge that if someone comes along to feed them just then, I get my head blown off.'

'There'll be a police marksman just behind you to fire right back,' Kirkstall told him.

'Thank you. That makes me feel much better. Why not use paralyzing darts?'

'Because they have to be fired from a gun and that makes a noise.'

'All right, so I dope the dogs without being killed. What happens then?'

'Your part is finished. You go back to the boat and we take over.'

Linus thought about that. It came out very pat and

sounded very easy. He tried to recall the access to Spit Bank.

'How do we know the dogs are going to be easily available? They might be deep in the bowels of the fort.'

Kirkstall shook his head. 'They live on the top. They've a kennel up there.'

Linus nodded. 'That's what I assumed: it would be the most obvious place to keep them. What I don't quite see is how we get that far. My recollection is that the steps from the landing stage led to a door into the fort but not at roof level. You're asking me to—what?—jump the equivalent of one storey on to a roof which slopes?'

'Not quite.' Kirkstall opened a folder and placed it in front of Linus. 'Look at these sketches. Over the doorway and projecting from the roof is a massive iron derrick. It's purpose is to lift the fort's launch out of the water by means of hawsers from a small bogie on the top of it. Safety railings run round the perimeter about a metre and a half from the outside edge. We have a man who will land with you, get up that hawser—which will be locked in position: it's only unlocked when a launch is being hoist up or down, in or out—and he will hook a rope ladder to those railings.'

'Without attracting the attention of those dread dogs,' Linus said sardonically.

'It should be possible. Our overflights suggest they spend most of their time asleep in the sun.'

'When a dog's sound asleep, his nose and his ears are still working. Especially if he has any pretensions to being a guard dog. They'd hear a seagull land—and if they didn't hear it, they'd smell it.'

'The alternative is to get a ladder attached to a grappling hook straight over the railings from the landing stage. Tricky from that angle,' Kirkstall said.

'And noisier. That really *would* wake them up,' Linus told him.

'Right. You've raised some problems. Good. Better to find out about them now than when we're in situ. I'll get the experts on to it. By the time we're there, they'll have sorted it out. Are you with us, Mr Rintoul?'

Linus thought about it. Common sense told him to say no, to go home and leave them to it, but if he did that, he might never know the full outcome and he couldn't deny the fact that he wanted to. He was also absolutely certain that unless he went along with them and was successful in coaxing the dogs to him, they would quite simply be shot, and that would be a great pity and an end they had done nothing to deserve. Besides, he had a fancy to see over March's home conversion.

'I'm with you,' he said. 'When does it happen?'

'Now.' Kirkstall handed him a notepad. 'Write down what you want in the way of drugs and they'll be waiting for you. We'll drive down straight away and be ready to go tomorrow morning, weather permitting.' Linus opened his mouth to speak, but Kirkstall held up a silencing hand. 'No need to pack a bag, Mr Rintoul. We'll provide you with appropriate clothes. Netley will get someone to phone MAFF in the morning and report you in sick. It's all in hand.'

'So it would seem,' Linus murmured. He had the uncomfortable feeling that, now that he had agreed to be roped in, events had acquired a momentum of their own, a momentum over which Kirkstall, whoever he was, might have some control, but Linus none, and if there was one thing Linus hated above everything else, it was the feeling that he didn't have control over his own life. He had a nasty suspicion that on this occasion that might prove to be quite literally true.

CHAPTER 10

The weather was glorious, the sky blue, the sea a flat calm. Or so the afficionados described it. Linus couldn't see how the words 'flat calm' could possibly cover all those little wavelets among which the small craft already out were bobbing about in a way that belied the term. Still, who was he to argue with the experts?

Netley and Cote, being members of the Thames Valley force, remained behind since the action was going to be in the province of the Hampshire constabulary, but Kirkstall and his still unnamed assistant had driven with Linus in a plain, unmarked car, some way behind the uniformed Woburn. Clearly Kirkstall wasn't Thames Valley.

'Are you Scotland Yard?' Linus had asked during the largely silent drive.

'You could say that,' was the reply, which Linus decided carried the corollary, 'but I wouldn't.' What did that leave him with? Special Branch? A term often bandied about but, to a layman, of imprecise definition. Linus considered pressing the point—he liked to know these things—but he decided not to. Kirkstall was far too adroit to tell him anything he didn't want him to know.

One place he hadn't expected to start from was HM Dockyard. Nor had he expected to be given a naval uniform. 'Is this legal?' he asked, turning it over gingerly.

'No need to worry about that,' Kirkstall told him. He, too, had become a rating.

'I thought we were going in plain clothes,' Linus persisted.

'Never a good idea to put all your cards on the table at once,' Kirkstall answered.

'True, but right now I'm more worried about the ones you've got tucked up your sleeve,' Linus retorted.

The choice of drug had been difficult because an instantaneous effect was required and most sedatives in general use didn't work that quickly. In the end and with great reluctance, Linus had decided to use Immobilon. If the dogs could be coaxed close enough to feed them a pill, which had been Kirkstall's original idea, they would be close enough to stick a needle in, and Linus knew that, in the hands of an experienced vet, that could be done without upsetting the dog. Animals are unaware that needles may hurt and therefore don't tense up in anticipation of pain, as people do. The needle could be in and out before the dog knew what had happened, and Linus had had enough to do with these particular individuals to be able to gauge the dosage reasonably accurately. He was more worried about himself. Immobilon could kill a man very quickly indeed. It was said to be the veterinary profession's favourite method of suicide. Carrying two loaded hypodermics while climbing a rope ladder was not Linus's idea of safety, even if he also carried the antidote and insisted that a further phial of Revivon was carried by someone else in the party. The Navy solved his problem by giving him a stout leather belt with pockets attached and even felt obliged to agree that, in the unlikely event of the top coming off a syringe, a needle was unlikely to penetrate the thick leather, his clothes and his skin. The risk was still there but it had been reduced to an acceptable minimum.

The launch was a naval one. Naval uniforms in naval launches anywhere in Portsmouth Harbour or the waters off Spithead occasioned even less comment than private craft and were much less likely to be challenged if March saw them and thought they were too close. Linus had seen the rope ladder tucked away beneath a tarpaulin and it seemed a very flimsy piece of equipment to have to scramble up, especially when a slip landed the climber in the notorious currents below. He was even less happy about the little cache of rifles that nestled beside the latter in the bottom of the launch and his confidence in the nature of this little expedition was further undermined by the observation that every member of the party except himself carried a sidearm. This was definitely not what he had envisaged.

He had thought the police had been unusually forthcoming in the information they had given him, even allowing for the fact that he, like them, was firmly bound by the Official Secrets Act. He was beginning to realize that, uncharacteristically open as they may have been about March's past, it had been nothing more nor less than the sprat to catch the proverbial mackerel—and he was the mackerel. They had been very far from open about what the mackerel would be involved in once it was firmly hooked and it began to look as if he wasn't going to like it one little bit.

As the launch dipped and rose through the sparkling waters of the Solent, Linus felt sick, and his nausea had nothing whatever to do with the little boat's progress through the choppy waves. The closer they came to the old fort, the more difficult their task seemed to him. He was sure Kirkstall had miscalculated, although nothing about the man would have led to a suspicion that he was anything other than exceedingly meticulous in his planning. The three-tiered landing-stage with flights of steps between each deck and two more to the side of the top deck, leading to the heavy oaken main door, was soon visible and the fort's launch hung suspended from the derrick.

So far, so good. What Kirkstall's plans took no account of was that the whole of this part of the fort was overlooked by what Linus could only call its domestic superstructure.

The top of the defensive walls was a deeply sloping concrete 'roof' and the superstructure itself was set back on the innermost part of this so that no one looking out of the wide windows would be able to see anything actually at the landing-stage because their view straight down would be impeded by the thickness of the defensive structure. They would, however, have a superb view of anyone climbing up to the derrick or crawling along its top, and although there was something which might have been a cable or perhaps a drainpipe going from the superstructure straight down the side of the fort which would provide someone more athletic than Linus with an easy route to the top, this, too, would be clearly overlooked as soon as the climber was above the vertical. There was an outside chance the first man to go might succeed in reaching the top before the occupants realized what was happening. It was highly unlikely the second one would, and the second one was to be Linus.

His trepidation increased as they approached and changed to bewilderment as they passed the fort in an arc that was clearly intended to take them right round it. His surprise must have shown in his face.

'I'm assured the navy frequently makes rings round one or other of the forts. Apparently it's good practice, though March has been known to complain about it. Doesn't like the sound of the engines. Says it spoils his peace.'

Which, Linus thought, was presumably why the sailor at the wheel cut the engine right back till it was doing little more than idle while giving him enough power to manœuvre the launch right up against the granite wall of the fort on the side opposite to the landing-stage, the derrick —and the superstructure.

'Be ready, Rintoul,' Kirkstall warned him. 'You're going up first.'

Linus stared at him. 'That wasn't the plan.'

Kirkstall grinned. It was as humourless a grin as the one

fixed permanently to any skull. 'It wasn't the plan we told you, no.'

'Then why . . .'

'Not now, for God's sake!'

'Now, or I don't go.'

'Because what you didn't know, you couldn't tell. OK?'

So much for trust and cooperation, Linus thought. I wonder what else I haven't been told.

A man stood up in the boat, a rope in his hand.

'Get it right first time,' Kirkstall hissed. 'There won't be a second chance.'

There was no acknowledgement from the man who was assessing the distance and the angle between the launch and the top of the structure. Linus, his gaze following that of the crewman, stared upwards. On this part of the fort, there were railings along the outermost edge. He knew then that his first assessment of Kirkstall had been correct. The man had done his homework thoroughly. He had just given Linus a completely different version—or, rather, an incomplete version. Linus's resentment grew.

The crewman—Linus had no idea whether he was a sailor, a policeman or something else—was weighing the end of the rope in his hand and Linus saw that a ball about the size of a cricket ball but apparently much heavier, had been spliced on to the end in a small snood of soft hemp. When the man judged that he had estimated weight, angle and distance correctly, he swung the ball round his head like a one-armed *bolas* and then let it fly to the railing. The sheer weight of the rope prevented it wrapping itself round and round the top rail. Instead it hung over, paused and slowly lowered itself and its rope downwards. Too slowly for Kirkstall's taste.

'For God's sake pull it faster,' he urged.

Someone grabbed the long-handled grappling-hook used to haul seamen out of the water and hooked it into the small snood as soon as it was within reach. The rope was pulled and as it went up and over the railing, the rope ladder which was attached to it rose swiftly into place and the end of the rope was firmly held by two crewmen.

Kirkstall turned to Linus. 'Got everything? Up you go.'

Linus stared at the flimsy, unstable ladder in horror. 'I've never been up one of these in my life,' he protested. It looked far worse in reality than it had sounded in theory.

'Then you need the experience,' Kirkstall said grimly. 'Don't worry. Someone'll be right behind you and we'll fish you out if you fall.'

If I don't crack my skull on the granite as I go, Linus thought bitterly.

He put his foot on the first rung and his other on the second. It felt even worse than it looked.

'Hurry,' Kirkstall hissed below him. 'We don't have all day.'

Linus took a deep breath. Maybe the secret was to go up as fast as you could. He tried. Apart from a disconcerting moment when the weight of the man behind him altered the 'feel' of the ladder, it seemed to be the solution and as he hauled himself up high enough to grab the railings, he had enough confidence to snap open the belt-purse containing his syringes. He glanced to either side and could just make out the shapes of the two Mastiffs curled up in the sun on the far side of the wall. He was not, as he had supposed, immediately opposite the superstructure but he would certainly be visible from it. It was perhaps fortunate that the windows affording panoramic views were on the seaward side. Those looking inwards were far more modest.

That was a problem he must bear in mind, though presumably the man behind him, whom a glance over his shoulder revealed was carrying one of those rifles, was presumably here to look after precisely that possible source of trouble.

The man's presence might be reassuring. The look on his face wasn't. His gaze was directed straight at the dogs. Great, Linus thought. They give me a marksman who's terrified of dogs. What use is that? Let's hope they stay asleep. He's going to be trigger-happy. I can feel it.

His instructions had been to coax the dogs to him. Fine. Except that despite all he had told Kirkstall, they were still sound asleep. Trust a dog to prove you a liar, he thought with the cynicism of experience. It did suggest they weren't the sharpest of guard dogs.

He had two choices, bearing in mind that speed was of the essence. He could make a deliberate noise. That would certainly wake them up and probably bring them running or, looking at their present somnolence, ambling over. The problem with that was that if they suddenly got up now to go and investigate something, there was a good chance that would alert someone inside the fort to the fact that something was up. His alternative was to creep over to them, trusting in Providence that no one looked out while he was doing it, and inject at least one of them while it still slept. He had no qualms at all about approaching the dogs. He reckoned he was far more likely to fall into the sea or be shot at from the superstructure than attacked by the two giants sprawled in the sun.

'What's the hold-up?' the man behind him whispered nervously, and Linus heard the bolt of his rifle pulled back.

'They're sound asleep on the far side of the fort,' Linus whispered. 'I can't very well call the blighters. The best thing will be to crawl along the top of the wall to where they are. That way I can anaesthetize one of them while he's still asleep. With any luck.'

'Too risky,' his companion said. 'You'll be seen.'

'Maybe. Keep your fingers crossed and pray—and keep your eyes on the windows opposite, not on the dogs.'

Linus clambered on to the wall. His original idea of

crawling along had to be abandoned: the seaward slope made it feel too unstable. It was easier to stand up and go on two legs. Because of the need to be inconspicuous, he crouched over as he went, oblivious of the fact that, since he was perfectly visible to anyone who glanced out in his direction, he might just as well have stood upright and been a lot more comfortable. He heard the other man surmount the railings. The metal of his rifle clinked gently against the rail. It was a slight sound but loud enough to bring the head of one dog up. Or perhaps it was the vibration through the hollow tubing that reached him.

'Sod it,' Linus heard him say. 'Bloody dogs.'

'Shh,' Linus said. 'They're OK. Leave him to me.' He reached into his purse and took out one of the syringes. 'Hello, old boy,' he said softly as the dog approached, head down to catch the full complement of smells from these intruders. Linus wondered briefly why yellow eyes always made a dog look ferocious. He cautiously—very cautiously—removed the protective plastic cover from the needle. 'How are you, then? Remember me, do you?'

'God almighty,' said the voice behind him. 'You don't have to hold a conversation with the bugger. Get on with it.'

'Don't tell your grandmother how to suck eggs,' Linus said in exactly the same placatory tone he was using to the dog. He knew the words didn't matter. The tone and his obvious lack of fear did. The damn fool behind him could upset all that. He held out his hand, the one that wasn't holding the syringe. Out of the corner of his eye he could see that the bitch had now woken up but she hadn't yet decided whether to follow her companion. Good. It meant their behaviour was unlikely to attract anyone else's attention. He remembered the names on the card outside their quarantine kennel. Tito and Tanya.

'Come on, then, Tito. Good boy,' he said. The dog was nearly within reach.

Linus was completely unprepared for the rifle shot that rang out from a point just to the side of his left ear. He jumped and the syringe tumbled from his hand, down the slope and into the sea. Tito dropped like a stone and a second report caught Tanya as she was half way to her feet, sending her over the edge with a resounding splash as her body hit the water.

Linus turned on the man furiously, oblivious of any danger.

'You bloody, irresponsible fool,' he shouted. 'What the hell do you think you're playing at?'

'They were dangerous,' the man said, his face stubborn. 'The other one was coming to attack. I had no choice.'

Linus pointed across to the superstructure. 'You had a choice. You were supposed to be watching my back—and not against dogs. That's what you were supposed to be watching. God, I've half a mind to use the other syringe on you, and that would be kinder than you deserve.'

Linus was unaware that the rest of the boarding party had landed during the commotion. He was aware that March and the discus thrower had emerged from a door at one side of the superstructure and he turned to face them.

'March,' he called out. 'I'm terribly sorry. This simply wasn't meant to happen. This . . . this half-witted, trigger-happy moron is frightened of dogs.' The scorn in his voice was far more devastating than any number of expletives would have been.

'Rintoul!' March's astonishment was scarcely surprising. 'What the devil are you doing here?' He wasn't pleased, either, though that was hardly unexpected. 'Who are all these people? What the hell is going on?'

'I was asked simply to put the dogs temporarily out of commission,' Linus told him, making his way round to where March and his minder stood. 'I'm afraid it's gone horribly wrong. These people—' he turned as he indicated those behind him and saw that they had fanned out round the perimeter of the fort and Kirkstall, his face a thunder-cloud of anger, was approaching. He no longer wore a naval cap and the trousers and jumper which were naval issue could just as easily be part of a police uniform. He held out his ID card.

'Kirkstall,' he said, snapping it back into his pocket before anyone could read enough of its contents to discover the source of his authority. 'I'm sorry about this, Mr March,' he went on. 'As Mr Rintoul says, things have gone rather wrong. I have a warrant to search this place. It will take some time, but you're welcome to accompany me to ensure that no damage is done.'

If ever a face snapped shut, it was March's, Linus thought. Devoid of expression, it was none the less cold and uninviting. For the first time Linus saw in his features something of the calculating character who had played along with his fellow Nazis while at the same time keeping the means to get himself out of the noose when the time came.

'I don't think you've done your homework, Mr . . . Kirkstall,' he said frostily. 'I have police protection against this sort of intrusion.'

'No, Mr March. You have protection in certain circumstances but those don't extend to your own breaches of the law.'

'Do you take me for a fool, man? If there is one thing I have always taken punctilious care not to do, it's to break the law. I don't know what information you think you have or what you think you're going to find, but you're mistaken. My hands are clean.'

Reflecting that the man would hardly be likely to say anything else, Linus was none the less inclined to believe him but he took the precaution of moving to one side so that he was no longer standing between Kirkstall and March.

'Do the names Miriam Greentree and David Huning mean anything to you?' Kirkstall asked.

'No, nothing. Should they?'

'They've been watching you very carefully for some time.'

March shrugged. 'So? That's the sort of thing you people are supposed to take care of.'

'We had our eye on them. They were . . . well, let's say precisely the sort of people you wouldn't want digging too deeply, given the circumstances.'

Linus thought March paled. He was quite sure the man knew exactly what Kirkstall meant and that the information was news to him.

'Which leaves me no nearer understanding why you've applied for a search warrant. If they've disappeared, I can assure you they're not here.'

'They haven't disappeared, Mr March. We know where they are. They're each in a morgue. One in Portsmouth and the other in Oxford. They've both been murdered.'

'Are you suggesting I did it?'

'I'm not suggesting anything, though for what it's worth, I don't imagine you pulled the trigger yourself. On the other hand, you do employ a minder and we have a shrewd idea of the weapon we're looking for.'

Linus was suddenly conscious of something pressing into the small of his back. He glanced over his shoulder to find the discus thrower standing there and, although he couldn't see that far over his own shoulder, he didn't delude himself that the man was pressing a finger into his spine. The man's voice in his ear was soft and barely audible. 'Right now I can destroy your kidneys and the spinal cord. You probably won't die.'

Linus didn't need the rest spelled out to him. Death would probably be preferable.

The man caught his arm and twisted it upwards before pulling him backwards. That was the first movement Kirkstall saw. He glanced quickly round and cursed to himself. Only one of the surrounding men had seen the movement and trained his rifle on 'John Smith'. The rest had been as immersed as he had been in the interchange with March.

'Call your dog off, March,' he said.

'My dog?' March glanced behind him, following the line of Kirkstall's gaze. 'What are you playing at, John?' His surprise when he saw the gun was unfeigned and he instinctively moved rapidly closer to Kirkstall. 'I didn't know he had that thing,' he said.

'Are you saying you didn't supply it?' Kirkstall asked, his mind rapidly considering whether he could deploy his men more advantageously and deciding he couldn't just yet, not while Smith had Linus.

'Would I be likely to give him one of those?' March asked scornfully. 'A Walther? German Army issue? I dare say if you get a close look at it, you'll find the Waffenamt mark. It's the last weapon I'd want to be associated with, believe you me.' He stared at his minder. 'Where did you get that thing? What are you playing at?' And then, after a silence during which it seemed various possibilities flicked through his mind, 'Who the devil are you, anyway?'

The young man was edging slowly backwards, taking Linus with him and Linus could hear the smile in his answer. 'John Smith, of course. Didn't you check out my credentials when you hired me? Even paid a firm of investigators to make sure, so why ask?'

March clutched at Kirkstall's sleeve, his calm suddenly gone. 'Shoot him. For God's sake shoot him,' he said.

'We're not risking Mr Rintoul's life,' Kirkstall replied. 'If you're getting nervous, why don't you work your way round the back of my men to the landing-stage. You'll find a launch there. The crewmen will look after you. Then we can get on with the job in hand.'

March glanced sideways at Linus and Smith who had by this time reached the protective casing over the central stairway that spiralled to the floors beneath.

Smith turned Linus round. 'Open it,' he commanded and Linus did as he was told.

March saw this and decided it was time to take Kirkstall's advice. He kept behind the encircling men and ran as fast as he dared along the sloping roof.

The discus thrower and his hostage disappeared through the door but the younger man's head reappeared almost immediately. So did his gun arm. He took the rapid, steady aim of the true marksman.

'Traitor!' he shouted and the word was almost lost in the report of the single bullet. Its impact hit March off-balance. His arms flailed in the effort to stay on his feet. One of the boarding party tried to grab him but the thrashing arms made it impossible and March, blood pouring down his side, finally over-balanced. His scream was silenced by the splash as the waters of Spithead closed over him.

Linus was a vet. His life had been spent dealing with bulls and boars and more than once it had depended on his split-second reaction to the menace of a dangerous and unpredictable animal. It served him in good stead now. For a few brief seconds the gun was no longer in his back and its user's concentration was focused on March. His grip on Linus's arm slackened.

Linus snatched himself away from the man's hold and raced down the spiral. He tried desperately to recall the layout of Spit Bank. He could hear the clatter of the other man's feet behind him. He guessed that the boarding party would be close behind the gunman but there was no room on those stairs for him to be overtaken and little scope for them to get a reasonable shot at him.

This worked in Linus's favour. It meant John Smith was similarly handicapped.

The entrance must be on the gun-floor below. The stairs had been opposite it.

To his horror, Linus discovered that Horse Sand was different. He could see no entrance and a fort converted to a house bore no internal resemblance to one in its original defensive layout. A sequence of doors opened on to the corridor that encircled the central well. He had no time to open them in the hope that one led to the entrance. The stairs continued to spiral down. The basement was probably used for cellerage and kitchens. He might not be able to get out of it, but at least he could play hide-and-seek until the boarding-party caught up with them.

He was completely thrown by encountering a luxuriously carpeted corridor. This was no basement. He could feel the first stirring of panic. He opened the door immediately opposite. A bedroom and very nice, too, by the look of it. A hiding-place? As he hesitated he caught sight of a flight of stairs descending from the adjacent passage.

These were not spiral and he was able to take them two at a time but a carpeted concrete floor carried neither sound nor reverberations from any pursuers. He must not forget that John Smith knew the layout.

Linus glanced back as he reached the bottom and glimpsed the gunman's plimsolled foot on the top stair.

He ran.

He knew he was in a shell passage. Somewhere it must link up at right-angles with a corridor running down the radius (if he were lucky, across the whole diameter) of the fort to the outside wall. There would be a bolt-passage. The guide at Spit Bank had said all the forts except St Helen's had one. He could hide there. He loathed the idea, but if he were able to hear running feet and if he kept enough distance between them, the curve of the wall would make it impossible for March's killer to shoot him.

He found the radial passage at last and was disconcerted when it was intersected by another circular corridor, too wide to be the bolt-passage. Horse Sand differed more than it had any right to. Pray God the guide had been right about its existence.

He had. The entrance to it was identical with a short flight of steps down to the door. More puzzlingly, there were two doors with a short stretch of masonry between them. Linus had no time to work out the possible implications. Safety lay in that narrow passage. He ran down the short flight of steps, turned the handle and slipped inside. The heavy door swung gently shut on silent, well-oiled hinges. The catch clicked.

Linus took a deep breath. Steady, he told himself. He waited for his eyes to become accustomed to the light, but there wasn't any light to become accustomed to. It was not reassuring. No sign of Smith, though. Better make sure of the exit, all the same.

He stretched his hand out to where the door was. He could feel the metal plate that must contain the locking mechanism but there was no handle, no catch, not even a key-hole.

Fine.

Great.

Don't panic.

Kirkstall and his men would be looking for him. Looking for both of them. Someone, somewhere must have a plan of this place. The military? The local planning authority? It must have some sort of listed status and March's alterations must have been approved. Finding those plans could take days, though. Outer walls of granite over Portland stone and inner walls of solid concrete were unlikely conductors of sound. No one would hear him shout.

The door had been pretty solid but he dared neither hammer on it nor shout. Not with a killer on the loose. Maybe he'd better get away from the door in case Smith came looking for him—or took refuge here himself. Since he wasn't here already, that was the most likely thing to happen. It looked as if Linus had succeeded in giving him the slip even though he couldn't quite work out why. After all, the man had been right behind him. Better to move away from the door.

Linus shivered. He couldn't open the door but that was where air and light lay, not in this claustrophobic hole. Still, the door felt different from the wall and he knew the passage went right the way round the fort so, if he kept one hand on the inner wall, he would have no difficulty getting back to the door again.

There had been two doors.

Why?

He stretched out his other hand. It encountered solid wall though, oddly, not cold wall. The passage was blocked.

His head told him it didn't matter. When he reached the other end, he just turned round and came back. It would make finding the door much easier.

Except that he wouldn't be able to evade a pursuer.

Perhaps the second door led into the other end of the passage. Perhaps, but it didn't make sense. Perhaps someone had constructed a storeroom. Linus decided this was much more likely, but it wasn't much help. Perhaps it meant that the passage was blocked on the side exactly opposite this one. Then there would need to be two doors. He didn't like the uncertainties. It looked as if he had painted himself into a corner.

What now?

It was becoming increasingly difficult to think straight. The total and absolute darkness coupled with the knowledge that he was in a very narrow tunnel frightened Linus more than he was prepared to admit. He could hear his heart beating unhealthily fast and he was having difficulty breathing. He slid down the wall till he was sitting against it, his knees up, his toes against the wall opposite.

He sat up straight. There was something behind him. Something warm. He felt. A narrow, warm pipe. He followed it along. It came out of the wall close to the door and ran along the bottom of the wall about two inches above the floor. For all he could tell, it went right round the inner wall of the passage. Central heating.

No one centrally heats a place they don't use.

There can't be many uses to which you can put a two-feet-wide passage.

Unless you're an art dealer.

Especially if you have pictures you don't want anyone to know about.

Like masterpieces stolen during the war.

Miriam was right. Maybe she was right by accident—he had little reason to doubt Kirkstall's word that she and Huning were Nazi hunters. Her story of the loot could have been made up to get him interested, or she could have known about it but it was incidental to their true purpose, and they just used it to to inveigle Linus in.

And if a man has a secret hoard of pictures, whether for his own satisfaction or to sell on, he's going to want to look at them from time to time.

And for that, he needs light.

The most probable place for a light switch was on the wall outside but it didn't necessarily follow. Linus stood up and ran his hand systematically down the wall beside the door. It took him a few seconds to work out that the switch, when he found it, was the sort that works on a timing mechanism and has to be pressed like a door bell. The light it gave was dim but adequate and with it, Linus's claustrophobia faded, though he was scarcely aware of this, all his attention being taken by what was on the walls.

March's hoard was secret, all right, and Linus devoutly hoped March was the only one to get any satisfaction from it. Hidden masterpieces it wasn't.

Carefully framed photographs, some of them well-known to Linus from newspapers and television documentaries, others new to him, mingled with rough sketches on fragments of paper. Everything carefully labelled. Occasionally individual names, often the year, always the location.

Belsen.

Auschwitz.

Theresienstadt.

Buchenwald.

God alone could know what sort of a person took them, let alone what went on in a mind that wanted them on its walls . . .

Suddenly the lights went off, their time finished. Now Linus knew real panic. It had been bad enough being incarcerated in a dark, narrow passage but at least he had believed it to be empty. It was much worse to know that he was surrounded by these ghastly reminders of the worst excesses of human degredation. Had there been switches at intervals along the walls? There must have been, but his attention had been too firmly drawn elsewhere to notice them.

Suddenly the lights went on and Linus was no longer alone. The discus thrower blocked his further progress and was grinning, gun in hand.

'How did you get here?' Linus asked. It was a superfluous question. He hadn't come in through the same door as Linus, so he must have come in the other one. Which meant the passage ran round the fort, uninterrupted except by that one wall. Linus couldn't see any immediate advantage to be gained from this realization but the more knowledge he had, the better.

'The other door. The cables come in from outside through the chamber between.' He nodded at the walls. 'Nice little collection, isn't it?'

Linus wondered at first whether the man was being ironic and a chill crept over him as he realized he wasn't. 'Charming,' he replied.

He began to edge his way back to the door. The only remotely good thing about his unwanted companion was that he must know how to get out of the passage from the inside. On the other hand, he was hardly likely to tell Linus. As he went, he noted the light switches at fairly frequent intervals. Good.

'Are you being sarcastic?' the gunman asked suspiciously.

Linus remembered the American accent foisted on to the German. Not a combination likely to appreciate British humour, but this was no situation in which to annoy him. 'Just a bit,' he said.

'You're not Jewish, are you?'

'Not remotely. Why?'

'You had Jewish friends. Made me wonder.'

Linus supposed March would have made sure his minder had similar tastes. 'It's not a crime, you know,' he said.

'It should be. In a civilized country it would be.'

There were limits to appeasement, Linus decided. 'You won't be surprised if I beg to differ.'

'Disappointed. Not surprised.'

At least the man hadn't taken umbrage. Linus ventured a bit further. 'Is this collection yours or his?'

'Oh, his. One of the few things I envied him.'

'You obviously thought alike. Why shoot him? And why call him a traitor?'

The question was a dangerous one. It put the man visibly on edge. Linus's eye was drawn to his trigger-finger. Would its tightening be noticeable to a highly interested observer? Probably not. Best to watch, all the same.

'Mr March was not a very nice man,' the gunman said in an unconscious echo of a previous description.

'So I believe,' Linus said mildly.

'Not to be trusted, either.'

'In business, you mean?'

'In business?' The man was momentarily puzzled. 'Oh, you mean your picture. No, he was straight enough in business, by all accounts. Did you know he had been a Nazi?'

'So I was told.' Linus glanced reluctantly around him. 'I'd have guessed, anyway,' he went on.

The man gave a short, humourless laugh. 'Yes, I suppose you would.' He paused. 'So am I.'

'I was beginning to think you might have sympathies in that direction.'

'Not sympathies. I am. I'm a fully fledged member of the Party.'

'Isn't it banned?'

'In some countries. Not in democratic ones like this.' He laughed. 'Ironic, isn't it?'

'Very,' Linus said truthfully. 'So why kill March? You obviously had a lot in common.'

The lights went out as he finished speaking.

'Behind you,' Smith said. 'Press the switch.'

Linus felt for the button and pressed it and then, as the lights came on, he pressed it again on an impulse to see whether that would switch them off again. It did. He pressed once more. 'Sorry,' he said. 'My finger slipped.' At least he now knew he could plunge the bolt passage into darkness. Pity he was no nearer learning how to get out of it. 'What about March?' he asked.

The young man's face clouded. 'A traitor. He was a Nazi before and during the War. He remained one afterwards though not openly. Given the normal course of events, he'd have hanged along with all the rest of those fighting for a better world. At least that would have been a martyr's death. A hero's, even. Instead he chose to save his own hide at the expense of his comrades-in-arms. He was a traitor to them, a traitor to his own beliefs and above all, a traitor to his Fatherland and the Third Reich.'

'Yes, I suppose that's how it must look from your point of view. Why work for him if that's how you see him?'

'I volunteered,' the gunman said proudly. 'It's taken the Party all these years to track him down. His footsteps were well covered. They needed someone to gain his confidence. There were many volunteers. I had the honour to be chosen, but I've failed.'

'Really? I should have thought you've been rather successful, all things considered. After all, March is dead—or so I assume. What I don't understand is why you haven't killed him before. After all, you've had plenty of opportunity since you started working for him, not just to kill him but to do so and get clean away afterwards. Yet you chose to do it today, here, in full view of goodness knows how many witnesses. Why?'

'My assignment wasn't to kill him. Once I'd made sure he was the right man, I had to get him out of England so that he could stand trial for his treachery. I only had the go-ahead to waste him as a last resort, if he looked like slipping through our fingers. My superiors knew they'd never get someone else as close to him as I'd managed to get and if I failed or things looked like falling apart, I had to use my discretion. I did.'

'Between you on the one hand and the organization behind Greentree and Huning, he didn't stand much chance, though, since he was a deeply suspicious man, I'm surprised he didn't suss you out. He sussed them all right.'

March's killer looked puzzled. 'He knew nothing about them. He didn't even realize he was being watched.'

'Didn't you kill them on his instructions?' Linus asked.

'No. I realized he was being watched and my contacts very quickly discovered who they were. The last thing the Party wanted was to have that lot whisk him out from under our noses to stand trial in Israel. I removed them. The man was a problem. We knew where to find him but we didn't know his name and it's always helpful to have a name when you want to lure someone into your territory. You gave us the name.' He laughed. 'You lured him away, too. At least, he thought it was you.'

That was a piece of information that made Linus very angry indeed but he schooled both his voice and his features so that the anger didn't show. 'Clever,' he commented.

The man grinned. 'That's what I thought.'

He was becoming increasingly cocksure. Linus wasn't sure whether this made him more dangerous or whether it was something he could turn to his own advantage, since it might mean the killer was less alert to the first signs of any counter-offensive.

Not that Linus had any strategy in mind. That was an area in which his mind was frustratingly blank. He played for time. 'What made you volunteer for the job? Did you have some sort of personal grudge against him? Or were you drafted into it?'

'Nothing like that,' the man said. 'Having a personal axe to grind can be a handicap—makes it more difficult to stay in control, to weigh up any odds dispassionately. I wanted the honour of being chosen. When I return, my mission successfully accomplished, my promotion in the Party, and in the Brotherhood in Styria, will be rapid.'

'Führer Smith?' Linus queried.

The young man shrugged modestly. 'It's a thought. But not Smith. I'll revert to Scheidegg.'

'Very wise. Tell me—did March ever get any Nazi treasures through his hands?'

John Smith—or Scheidegg—looked bemused. 'Not that I know of,' he said. 'This would be the place for it, I suppose, but he didn't take that sort of risk. No. Assembling this little lot was risk enough.'

'Did he bring them in himself? In the false bottom of that vehicle?'

The man shrugged again. 'I didn't discover everything, you know, but I shouldn't think so. How could he? He was only protected while he stayed in Britain. No. He paid generously and the sort of person who has this sort of thing to sell meets enough weirdos not to think them odd any more.'

'Weirdos? Doesn't that make you one? After all, you've admitted you envy him this collection.'

The killer thought about it. 'No. If the subjects were Aryan, that would make us weirdos. They're not. We're normal.'

This was a line of reasoning so lateral—and so obscene—that Linus gave up on it. The time spent talking had, however, paid off. He realized that an earlier question was now being answered in reverse. He wasn't sure how much noise from this side of the door could be heard outside but sounds were filtering through in the other direction. They were faint and indeterminate but they were there. The best guess was that the boarding party had reached the basement.

The easiest way of attracting their attention would be to persuade John Smith, or whatever his name was, to fire his pistol. Unfortunately Linus couldn't think of any other probable target than himself, and the man was no amateur shot. Still, it was worth a try.

He held up one finger. 'Shh. What's that?'

They listened in silence for one, maybe two, seconds. Seconds when the gunman's attention was on the noises outside, not what was going on in the passage.

Swiftly, Linus pressed the light button, simultaneously throwing himself sideways as the killer's knee-jerk reaction was to fire at the spot where he had last seen him.

The flash briefly lit the passage and the simultaneous report quickly followed by another reverberated in the narrow space.

Linus clapped his hands over his ears to no effect. He thought he heard a scream but it was difficult to be sure. He wasn't even sure it wasn't his own scream he heard. He could think of nothing except the excruciating pain in his ears, pain from which there was no respite.

He couldn't hear the door being opened and was only imperfectly aware of a man stepping over him as he writhed on the floor and another one helping him to his feet and out into the ante-room beyond. He tried to stand but his knees buckled under him and he would have fallen sideways had someone not supported him.

'His balance has gone,' someone said but Linus couldn't hear them through the noise that still reverberated inside his head.

'Get him to the launch and make sure an ambulance meets you,' Kirkstall said. 'We'll use the fort's launch if you're not back.' He stepped inside the passage where the young Nazi lay scrunched up across the narrow space, a rifle pointing at him from either side.

'Dead, sir,' one of the men said.

'Turned it on himself?' Kirkstall asked.

'Shouldn't think so, sir. Looks as if it was a ricochet.'

'Good. Saves a lot of public explanations if it is. Get him out.' He glanced round the walls. 'Jesus Christ Almighty,' he said.

One of the men followed his gaze and crossed himself. 'Amen to that, sir.'

The ringing in Linus's ears persisted for several days, making it difficult always to hear what was said to him in the naval hospital where he had the luxury of a private ward. He suspected that he owed this privilege more to the secret nature of the March affair than to any respect for his part in it. He was allowed no visitors, though, and since he also received no cards, he guessed no one had been told where he was. He would quite like to know himself but the nurses were singularly unforthcoming.

Kirkstall came to see him on the fifth day. 'How're you feeling?'

The ringing had diminished to bearable proportions. 'Broadly speaking and taking things all round, I'd say bloody sums it up quite well,' Linus replied.

Kirkstall smiled. 'You'll be out of here in a couple of days. The certificate that's gone to MAFF says 'flu, by the way.'

'Signed by my own doctor or another? I do need to know,' he pointed out.

'True. Let's say it won't cross their minds it's anything other than your GP. That's what I'm here for: to remind you that you've had 'flu. You don't talk about this to anyone. Not to your son, your aged mother or the fancy piece you happen currently to share your bed with.'

'Chance would be a fine thing.'

'Nevertheless, don't. HM Government would find it distinctly embarrassing. Tell me, why didn't you think to use that second hypodermic on him? It would have saved a lot of trouble.'

Linus stared at him. 'The second hypodermic? Good God, I'd forgotten all about it. What a fool!'

'Not at all—just a man whose first reaction to danger

isn't to kill the source of it. In my line of business it's rather reassuring to meet one.'

'What exactly *is* your kind of business'?' Linus asked him. 'Special Branch? MI5?'

Kirkstall managed a smile which contained not a vestige of humour. 'You don't need to know that.'

Linus sighed. 'Very well, then, but given that this is all so very hush-hush, can I have the answers to some other questions?'

'You can ask. I'll answer if I can.'

'What happened to the minder?'

'Very convenient, as it happened. He fired two bullets in the passage. One of them ricocheted off the wall and through his eye. It killed him.'

'It would. You're sure that's what happened?'

'If that's an oblique way of asking me if we bumped him off, no, we didn't.'

'And March? Did the bullet kill him?'

'No, but the Solent did. He drowned before we could fish him out.'

'What happens to his collection?'

'That's out of my control. I imagine it'll be destroyed. Either that or hidden away under top security wrappers.'

'Isn't there a Holocaust Museum in Israel somewhere?'

'Couldn't release it without embarrassing explanations. It just goes to show, though.'

'Show what?'

'That the leopard can't change his spots.'

'Nor the Ethiope his skin,' Linus murmured, 'though I doubt if *that's* a comparison a Nazi would appreciate. There's just one other thing. If things hadn't turned out the way they did, how the hell would I have got out of that passage? There was no internal release catch on the door.'

'There was on the other one. All you had to do was to walk right round.'

'But why? Why a catch on the one and not the other?'

'When our experts analyzed that nasty little exhibition, they found it was arranged chronologically and within the chronology, alphabetically. If you went in at the beginning, as you did, you walked round and came out at the end. No need for a two-way catch on your door. Very methodical people, the Germans.'

'But not, thank God, methodical enough to organize a Thousand-Year Reich,' Linus told him.

Kirkstall reached into his pocket and brought out a bottle of twenty-year-old malt and reached over for Linus's glass. 'We can both drink to that,' he said. 'Water with it?'

Linus stared at him. 'And I thought you had no sense of humour,' he said. 'I did you an injustice. Just double the dose, if you don't mind.'